THE GHOST DEER

THE SAWTOOTH LEGACY

BOOK ONE

R.B. MOLLER

The Ghost Deer

Copyright © 2022 R.B. Moller

ISBN PB: 979-8-9863815-0-3

Library of Congress Control Number: 2022919334

Illustrations by R.B. Moller and Melody Moller

Published by Lifting Tree, LLC

www.liftingtree.com

THE GHOST DEER

THE SAWTOOTH LEGACY

BOOK ONE

R.B. MOLLER

Lifting Tree

www.liftingtree.com

ACKNOWLEDGMENTS

To my dad, brother, and son, who have taught me the meaning of adventure and that one's character of fortitude is not given, it is grown...

~

With much gratitude to my wife, children, parents and family for their unending support, feedback, and encouragement.

A special thanks to my daughter Melody Moller for her contributions to the illustrations and all those who provided valuable input.

A big thank you to Caleb Turner for proofreading. And with sincere appreciation to Variance Author Services and Tim Schulte as well as Brian Mlambo from ICHD Designs for the cover design, and for Tim's depth of experience and exceptional efforts in editing, design and directing the publication of this work.

PROLOGUE

Whether the buck was a ghost or a deer, I'll never know.

To some, this story might seem a tall tale, suitable to hang in the hallways of legend, fit for the realms of folklore and fantasy. Some have called it a 'dream,' and others a 'wild story of imagination.' Yet to me—it is very real. I'll leave that for you to decide.

CHAPTER 1

THE SIGHTING

SAWTOOTH MOUNTAINS, CENTRAL IDAHO,
JUNE 24th, 1987

A branch snapped in the dense undergrowth, and I was close enough to hear the creature breathing. Inching forward, my hands sank into cool, moss-covered earth that smelled of decayed leaves and rotting wood. Water seeped into a deep cloven hoof print as big as my hand. Seconds passed as I stared in disbelief.

This must be an elk. I wish Dad were closer.

I knew he was just sixty yards away at the top of the ridge, glassing the ravine for mule deer, but it felt like a mile.

Knees wet, I repositioned myself, straining to see through the wall of branches smothering my view. A loud snort pierced the air. I dropped to my stomach. Small saplings swayed back and forth on the other side of the brush, accompanied by scraping sounds and snapping twigs. I laid my head on the ground, trying to become one with the soil. With courage, I slowly rose to my knees struggling to control my breath, hoping the creature's noise would cover my movement.

I wish this wasn't a scouting trip! I cursed inside, agonizing that my first bow hunt was still over two months away.

With only my arms, I dragged my body forward inch by inch, craning my neck through the thinning branches. A massive white animal rubbed against the tree in front of me. I froze. *Could this be the legendary muley buck Grandpa told stories about?* Sweat trickled down my forehead as I wiped my eyes.

Suddenly, something crawled into my ear, and searing pain followed. Jerking back, I swatted it away, stopping the hornet's attack. There was a loud *"snort,"* then *"thump, thump, thump!"* I bolted to my feet, frantically scanning the forest as a flash of white fur and a web of antlers disappeared into the trees.

"Noooo!" I yelled.

In pursuit I ran, dodging rock and brush. Branches clawed at my face and arms.

I've got to get another look; I just have to!

Dad called out from above. "Tater! You okay?"

I cut across a meadow, running at full speed for the patch of pines where the buck had disappeared. Upon rounding the corner, I skidded to a stop. A pine bough swayed back and forth as if waving goodbye, while the squirrels chattered—laughing at my defeat.

CHAPTER 2

THE BET

THOMPSON FAMILY RANCH, CENTRAL IDAHO,
JULY 2nd, 1987

The creaking door slammed. "Tater T. Thompson! You know I don't like you running out like that!" Mom yelled through the open kitchen window, dishes clanging in the background.

"Sorry Ma... off to Grandpa's!" I said, leaping from the porch stairs.

Partway down the dirt path to the front gate, she grabbed me with the dreaded words, "No, you don't! Not now, young man. You haven't had your supper! Come on back and get your chores done while I finish up the potatoes."

"But I already did!" I said, dreading what was coming next.

"Did you now?"

"Yeah, I slopped the hogs and cleaned the horse stalls like you asked me to."

"Did Dad check your work?"

I brushed back the hair from my eyes, stood up straight and pulled on the straps of my torn overalls. "Ah, Mama," I protested. "Come on now, he doesn't need to keep after me all the time. I'm over thirteen years old an' been doing this ever since I was a boy."

Mom stopped washing the dishes and leaned out the windowsill. "You act like you're a grown man."

"Well—I am!" I defended, stomping my foot. "You know I'm going hunting with the guys this fall. Dad wouldn't take me if I couldn't keep up. He says the days are long and the mornings are early. Sounds like man's work to me."

"What about your dinner? You can't expect to keep living off Grandma's biscuits."

"I'll be fine. I'm too busy, anyway. Got to talk to Gramps about the Ghost Deer."

She laughed. "Too busy? You sound just like your father. Sometimes I think he married these cattle. This ranch

5

keeps him going from sunup to sundown." Leaning out the window, she eyed me over. Then, looking back at the kitchen, she sighed. "Alright, don't let Grandpa fill your head with too many of those stories of his. You run along now, be home by dark."

"I will!"

Opening the gate, I slapped my thigh. "Come on, Bandit! See if you can keep up," I said, swinging my leg over my bent bike.

Bandit stood from his worn spot on the front porch and stretched, looking back with longing at the front door. It was apparent he'd rather stay for dinner, but his loyalty was unwavering. He loped down the stairs and lumbered up alongside me, licking my hand.

I had been romping around with Bandit as long as I could remember. Mom said I would tug on his ears when I was just a little tyke, back when Dad's cowboy boots came way up my thigh. He always let me do it without a whimper or a growl.

An old Blue Heeler, Bandit was gray and tan, with a faded black patch over his left eye. Dad had gotten him years ago to help herd the cattle on the ranch. His medium build, pointed ears and attention to detail made him well suited for the work.

As Bandit got older, the hard miles and long days got too much for him. Because of this, Dad got a new pup and trained her to take Bandit's place. After that, he let the old rascal pal around with me at the homestead.

Mom said Bandit always missed me when I went out with Dad to help drive cattle. Starved for excitement, Bandit dug out every ground critter within miles. Mama liked him for keeping the mice down, but sure would complain about all the holes and the barking at night.

He kept a good watch on the place too, driving coyotes away from the chicken coop. The problem was, when he was just a pup, he didn't keep himself from those cackling hens. Which is how he got his name, Bandit. That, and the black patch over his left eye, which made him look like a robber. With time, the dark patch faded to gray. His face was now white with years, but his heart was still gold as ever.

As I pedaled down the dirt road, Grandpa's farm emerged on the horizon. Bandit trailed to the side with his tongue hanging out. The old boy had long since learned he didn't enjoy eating dust and kept clear of it.

It always bothered me that between our well-kept ranch and Grandpa's farm was the Bogsleys'. I shook my head as I passed. Their fields of hay and grain were now wild grass and sagebrush. The farmhouse looked more gray than white, the exposed wood rotting more each year. The handrailing on the front deck was broken out in several places, and the shingles looked like curled-up potato chips, with the roof sagging on one side.

Rusted-out cars littered the front yard, and a half-torn-apart tractor was parked on the side. Their picket fence sagged under its own weight. At the end, the post broke off, twisting the fence into the ground.

I didn't understand why, but I never saw their father around much. When I did, he always looked angry. He had a bad limp on one side, and despite Dad's efforts to help, he would have none of it.

Dad said Mr. Bogsley had gotten hurt several years ago in a farming accident. Between the money drying out and the bitterness of a life gone sour, their mama left him.

The boys stayed with their dad and got meaner every year. Reed Bogsley, sixteen, and Parley, fourteen, were like rattlesnakes on my heels. Every chance they got, they tried to find some way to make my life miserable.

As Bandit and I neared their home, I said, "Let's go, boy!" He knew what to do. I stood and cranked on the pedals so hard I thought I might rip them off. Bandit always hated this part. With his age, he wasn't much for running, but he clearly remembered what would happen if he didn't.

The thing I hated about late summer was the dirt was loose and the dust was high. This put a pile of hurt on my efforts to speed past those troublemakers without detection.

9

Suddenly, my bike dropped into a rut. Attempting to keep my bent tire pointed straight, I fought the handlebars like a long-horned steer. After breaking free of the distraction, I frantically scanned side to side, probing every pile of junk in their yard.

The front door hung quiet, and I strained to hear any noise from the house. The tall grass hummed with grasshoppers, a meadowlark sang a sweet melody, and leaves rustled in the distance. I caught a whiff of cut hay coming from Grandpa's farm, flooding my mind with memories.

A good day!

As the Bogsleys' house drifted from view, I eyed down the massive cottonwood trees lining the road, trunks as big as tractor tires.

Grateful, I nodded my head, letting go of one handle. I turned to look back. "We did it, Bandit!" I said. "In the home stretch now—come on, boy! Keep up!"

Instantly, something thin and rigid slammed into my chest, knocking me off my bike into the dirt. Bandit growled, coming alongside. I couldn't breathe. Every bone in my back screamed. Dust clouded around me as I coughed, holding my ribs. It felt like a metal rod had slammed across my chest.

Someone laughed. Footsteps neared. "You thought you slipped on by, didn't you?" Reed Bogsley said.

Other footsteps came from the edge of the road. Bandit growled, moving closer until he was standing over me. "You little rat!" Parley said, kicking dirt in my face. "You mean to tell me you thought you could just stride across our property easy as you please?"

Rolling over, I covered my face with my hands and coughed. Gasping for breath, I struggled to my knees, keeping pressure on my chest with my arms, attempting to ease the pounding pain. Reed held a rope wrapped around a big cottonwood that now lay in the dirt extending across the road.

"Hah, you fell right into our trap! I told you, Parley, didn't I? It knocked him flat."

My legs were weak and my hands shook with adrenaline as I fought the pain required to stand. I spat out dirt and attempted to clear my dry throat. "Why don't you leave me alone? I'm tired of you always trying to find new ways to hurt me. I have a right to travel this road. You don't own it!"

Parley laughed, brushing back his tangled, dusty blond hair from his eyes. "Now, what fun would that be?" he said, revealing his yellow teeth.

Reed's dark brown eyes glared down at me, hard and piercing. "Heard you've seen a white buck. From what they say, big as an elk! Now, why don't you tell us where to find him? We'll take care of him for you, nice and tidy like."

"I will not!" I said, straining to keep my quivering lip in check. "I found the Ghost Deer. The Old Muley is mine to hunt. Dad and I spent a ton a time scouting him out. Find your own buck!"

Reed grinned, his gaze cold. "I figured you might say that." Through gritted teeth, he said, "Now why would I want to go to all that trouble when I can just—ask—you?"

As Reed moved closer, Bandit revealed his fangs, giving a deep warning growl as he stepped in front of me.

"Now there, no need to get excited," Reed said, extending his arms towards Bandit. "We're just having ourselves a talk among friends." Bandit barked, snapping at Reed's open hand, making him jump back.

Parley moved in front of me. Though only a year older, he had me by two inches and twenty pounds. "Tell us about this buck you saw, Rat," he said. "You're just spewing a bunch of lies to get attention. There's no such thing as a white mule deer."

"Am not! I saw a monstrous white buck. He could be older than any of us. I'm going to hunt him this year, find him too. Who knows, I might even bring him home."

"You get a good look at him?" Reed asked.

"Not a good look," I said, lowering my head. "A flash of white and some big prints is all I saw."

"See… You didn't see him." Parley said. "You don't even know how many points he has. And here you are going around telling a bunch of hog slop."

He had me there. I hadn't gotten a good view of him. It all happened so fast. At a glimpse, he sure looked like a mule deer, with a towering rack. *Had my mind been playing tricks?* No, I'd seen the tracks, even showed them to Dad. Something was out there alright, something I'd never encountered.

13

"Goin' bow hunting?" Reed asked, pointing his finger at me.

"I sure am," I said, rubbing my aching chest.

"Hah, even if you saw him, you'd never get a shot. A buck like that would run circles around you. You haven't even been hunting before, have you?"

I lowered my head, shaking it from side to side.

Reed looked at me with pity and chuckled. "You're just a baby. I doubt you'll even get a buck at all. You don't have any idea what you're getting into, expecting to bring home a deer on your first bow hunt... Hah!"

"I've been practicing!" I fired back.

"Yeah, prove it!"

"What do you mean?"

"Since you're so confident you'll get a buck, I bet you don't even get a little fork horn."

"Will too!"

Reed threw the end of the rope at me, and it stung as it lashed across my neck. I flung it off. Bandit barked, forcing him back.

"You're nothin without that dog!" Reed said, spitting at Bandit. "If we ever catch you without him, you'll be wishing you lived in another county."

"Hey, I know!" Parley said. "Why don't you bet the dog?"

"Bandit?"

"Yeah, if you're as good a hunter as you say you are. You wouldn't have any problem at all giving us that dog there if you don't get a buck this year—would you now?"

"I'm not betting Bandit!"

"Just what I thought, a yellow-bellied ground squirrel. Go hide in your hole!" Parley said, folding his arms.

"I'm not hiding!"

Reed laughed. "Sure looks like it to me."

I grabbed hold of my overall straps, biting my lip. "What's in it for me?"

"Ah, why not!" Reed said. "If you get a lucky shot and bring home a buck, we'll leave you alone until this time next year."

"First of July?"

"Yeah, you calling me a liar?"

"No, just checking."

Reed wiped sweat from his forehead, brushing back his dark hair. "What you need to understand, boy, is Bandit is going to be ours after the hunt. You got it?"

"Yes—I got it," I said hesitantly, wishing I'd caught the words before leaving my mouth.

Reed thumped his fist into his hand. "You go back on this deal, we'll still get payment!" Giving me a sinister grin, he poked me in the chest, right where it still hurt. "I reckon he's got a few years left in him. I could use me a good huntin dog."

Hesitating, I looked at Bandit's loyal eyes staring up at me. A year without torment sounded like Heaven. I was confident I would harvest the Ghost Deer, or at least bring home a young fork horn.

"Well, what do you say?" Reed asked, spitting on his hand and holding it out. "I'm tired of waiting! Do we have a deal?"

"Come on!" Parley prodded. "You wimping out on us?"

"Do we have a deal?" Reed insisted, shaking his extended hand.

My head burned as sweat streamed down my face. I was sick of being tormented. Any relief sounded nice. I looked at Bandit. "We'll show 'em boy, won't we?" I whispered.

"What you sayin?" Reed demanded.

"I'm going to get a buck, maybe even the white muley. When I bring one home, you'll be leaving me alone. You got that?" I asked, extending my hand.

"Yeah, whatever..." he replied, smirking. "I'll be looking forward to having me a dog, come end of hunt."

Pain exploded through my hand as he gripped it.

CHAPTER 3

FREEDOM

Later that evening, as I sat on the front porch steps listening to the crickets chirp, I stroked Bandit's head. A gentle breeze blew from the west, rustling the large maple trees in my grandparents' front yard. The warm butter and raspberry jelly covering Grandma Thompson's hot biscuit melted in my mouth, and I treasured every bite.

The bet I'd made with the Bogsleys tormented me. Mom always taught me not to gamble, and here I was risking my best friend. I knew if it came down to it, I could choose to withhold Bandit from those menacing brothers. But I believed myself to be a man of my word, and I would have to keep it.

The front door creaked as Grandpa Silas Thompson stepped out. "How you doin, Tater?" he asked, standing alongside me. "From what Grandma said, sounds like you had quite a run-in with the Bogsley boys a bit ago."

"Yeah, I did."

"How are you feeling?"

"Alright—my chest and back still hurt, but I'll be okay."

Grandpa sighed and plopped down on the bench next to the house. He removed his John Deere hat and wiped sweat from his forehead. "The evening breeze sure feels good after a long day in the fields."

I nodded in agreement.

"Tater, sit with me for a spell," he said, patting the bench. "I know how your mom likes you home before dark. I won't keep you long."

Grandpa's kindness was unmatched. I could talk to him, and he'd listen. It seemed like he always knew exactly what to say to help me feel better and see life as I should. His mustache and flannel checkered shirts were as timeless as I could remember, as were his strong, weathered hands. He wasn't that old, but he was getting older, and with each year, he seemed to slow down.

I stood up from the porch steps and joined him on the bench. Bandit followed me, sitting at my feet.

"Grandpa?"

"Yes, what is it? Something playing on your mind?"

"Well—I messed up today."

"How's that?"

"I'm not sure how it happened, but one thing led to another and I ended up betting Bandit," I said, rubbing my dog's head. "I told the Bogsleys they could have him if I didn't get a buck this year."

He sat in silence for a moment. What I thought he might say was, "*Now, why would you do a thing like that?*" But that's not what he said.

He put his arm around my shoulder. "I see. So, what are you going to do about it?"

"I don't know Gramps; get a buck, I guess. I shouldn't have made the bet, especially with it being old Bandit here. But they promised to leave me alone for a whole year. After I'd just got beat up by them again, I couldn't pass it up. They boxed me into a corner."

"A corner it is," he said, nodding. "There's a mighty good thing about a corner, though."

"What's so great about being cornered?" I asked, folding my arms.

"There's only one way out."

"I guess you're right," I agreed.

"The hard part is finding that way out, Tater."

"What do you mean?"

"You have to turn around."

"Turn around? Shouldn't I fight my way through it? Turning around seems like running, Grandpa."

"It's like this—as long as you're looking into the corner, there *is* no way out. You can run all you want, you can fight all you want... and not move at all. In fact, the harder you drive into that corner, the more cornered you'll be."

"How does this work for me?" I asked. "What do I need to do to turn around?"

"You have to get a new perspective on the situation. As soon as you do, a whole world of opportunity opens."

"So, you're saying there *is* a way out of my bet?"

"There is, but if you want to keep your promise, it's the only way. You'll have to get yourself a buck this fall."

"How can I guarantee getting a buck, Grandpa? There's so much at stake..."

He chuckled and patted me on the knee. "It's going to be alright, Tater. If I know you even half as well as I think I do, you'll talk one of those antlered critters into sitting next to you in the truck on the way back if you have to."

"I don't know. Those Bogsleys treated me like a flat-out liar the way they teased me about the Ghost Deer. They think I don't even know what I'm doing—like I'm just a greenhorn!"

"Is that what you believe?"

"No, I don't think so..."

I ran my hand through my hair and sighed. "Anyway—I guess I don't know anymore."

"Tater, let me tell you something. What you choose to believe is important. In fact, what *you* tell yourself will impact your life more than everyone else combined. You hear me?"

"Yeah, I guess…"

I looked down at Bandit's big brown eyes gazing up at me.

You believe in me boy, don't ya? I thought, as I scratched him behind the ear.

Then a thought struck me like a thump on the head. *What am I thinking!? Here I went and got clobbered by those bullies for a question I haven't even asked.*

"You've seen him, Gramps, haven't ya?"

"Who, Tate?"

"You know, the Ghost Deer."

"The ghost what?"

"Yeah, that's what I call him. He was huge! Big as an elk with a rack of antlers like none I've ever seen."

"Oh yeah, the white buck… Your Dad mentioned you'd seen something of the sort."

"Yeah, Gramps... I reckon with how much time you've spent trailing these mountains, you've chased him around plenty of times."

"Now hold on, Tater. Sure, I've seen some big bucks up in these hills over the years. Some I'd have been mighty proud to bring on home. One buck—the King, as we called him—was something extraordinary. Not a white one, though, not like what you're talking about."

I looked at him with pleading eyes. "You sure? I thought for certain he was the one."

He smiled warmly and sighed. "Now don't get me wrong, I've heard some talk in town. It's just hearsay, mind you. Old Bob Gunnison swore by it. A good man. He's always done right by me, but everyone else thought he was crazy. He died several years ago and no one could ever prove his claims. The way I figure, it must have been an extra dose of buck fever."

My eyes got all wet and blurry. "You believe me, don't ya, Gramps?"

He rubbed the back of his neck. "Uh—yeah, sure I do, Tater. I wouldn't have a reason not to. You just keep your hopes up, you hear? We'll have to see if we can find that old muley again." He grinned. "Might just give him a real wallop," he said, thumping his fist into his thick hand.

Against my best efforts, my voice cracked as I fought the emotion exploding inside. "But what if we can't? What if I fail, Grandpa? Then what? I'll lose Bandit... I'll lose everything!"

"No guarantees, Tater. Just remember, the only part you have control over is whether you choose to quit or to keep trying. You're the master of your thoughts and actions—not the Bogsleys or anyone else. What you choose to think will control what you choose to see, and what you choose to see will rule what you choose to do."

Looking down, I sighed. "I wish it were easier," I whispered.

"You ponder about that. When this hunt is through, you may find you've won more than freedom from the Bogsleys. You may very well find you've found freedom from the prisons inside yourself."

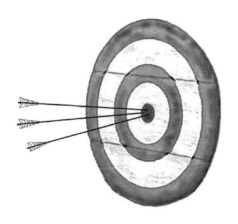

CHAPTER 4

BULLS EYE

THOMPSON FAMILY RANCH, CENTRAL IDAHO,

JULY 12th, 1987

The bowstring twanged as my arrow spiraled through the air, sinking deep into the cardboard bullseye hung in front of the straw bales behind our home. I pulled another arrow from my quiver, inspecting the tightness of the tip. Nocking it, I drew back and released.

"How about that shot, Bandit?" I asked, scratching him behind the ears. "Those deer don't have any idea what's coming." He licked my hand and looked up at me. "Yeah, we'll get that buck and keep those greasy Bogsleys off our tail for an entire year."

"What do you mean, off your tail?" Dad said, coming up through the rustling knee-high grass behind.

"Oh, sorry—just talking to Bandit."

"The Bogsley boys been trouble?"

"Yeah, but it's nothing I can't handle," I said, lowering my head as I rubbed the back of my neck.

He folded his arms, giving me a probing look. I wanted to tell him about my bet and how I had gotten in over my head, but I didn't think he'd handle it well. Though he was my dog now, Bandit had spent much of his life riding around with Dad in the truck and herding cattle. If Dad knew I'd put one of his best friends up for a bet, it wouldn't sit well.

"Looks like you're doing good," Dad said, pointing. "Five out of six arrows—dead center."

"Yeah, I'm doing alright at twenty yards. I still struggle at thirty, though."

"That's alright, keep practicing. You'll get it. There's a month and a half before opening day. Need to nail down the forty-yard range as well..."

I nodded. My stomach sank as I realized how far I had yet to go. *What had I done? Why was I so sure I could get a buck on my first hunt?*

"Mom's got supper on. Come inside and get some grub," Dad said, gripping my shoulder with his heavy, work-hardened hand.

When I didn't move, he snatched up a long strand of field grass, chewing on the soft end. "Well, Tate, what do you say?"

"I'm not hungry. My stomach's upset," I said, kicking at the dirt.

"Mom's made potatoes and gravy—your favorite, I believe?"

He had me there. They hadn't nicknamed me Tater for nothing.

"Alright—I'll be right in."

Dad took off his cowboy hat and used his sleeve to wipe the sweat from his forehead. "Good; make sure you thank your mother. She's been to a lot of work."

I looked up at his wiry silhouette shading me from the late afternoon sun and nodded.

Shortly, I sat at the table with mom, dad and my two sisters, Sarah and Molly. The smells of hot rolls, roast beef and potatoes drifted through the air, making my mouth water.

After saying a blessing on the supper, Dad handed me the bowl of potatoes. "I've got some good news, Tate," he said, smiling. "Uncle Sam and his boys are joining us on the hunt this year."

"Really, Dad!?"

"Yup, be here for the bow hunt."

Now, the hunting bug had bitten me for as long as I could remember. I'd dreamed of having adventures like my older cousins, Brock and Carter, ever since they started telling me stories. I considered them mountain men, and my uncle Sam... the legendary Daniel Boone himself.

This might help my chances, I thought. *With them as guides, bringing home a buck just got a lot better.*

"They'll be driving all the way from Wyoming, so they'll miss the first day's hunt, but they'll join us that night," Dad said.

Although I was excited, fear crept in. I'd been to their home and seen the walls covered with trophy deer, elk, and moose racks, even an antelope or two. Not only would they be a great help to my chances—they might just end up with the Old Muley themselves.

"I sure hope you're going to be safe, Tater," Mom said. "I've heard some crazy stories over the years, and I'm quite aware how tired your dad is when he gets home. Don't want you going off and getting hurt."

"I'm not a baby anymore, Mom. I'll be just fine; you'll see."

"I sure hope so," she said, glancing over at Dad, eyes narrowed. "Rod, you go easy on him."

He nodded. "I'll take good care of him, Hannah. He'll be alright—no worries now."

Sarah, my older sister, glared at me. "Tater, I don't know why you would even want to hunt those poor innocent deer. They're too cute to be shooting, and I love watching them in the fields."

"Now, why are you giving me a hard time about that?"

Brushing crumbs off her pink dress, she sat up straight. "Well, they are! Brock and Carter's stories about shooting all those beautiful animals drove me crazy growing up."

"You're eatin beef, aren't ya?" I fired back. "You think them smelly old cows are cute too?"

"Now, now," Mom said. "No need to be arguing about something like that. If those boys want to jerky out the deer and have a few steaks on the side, that's fine by me."

"I like deer venison too," Molly said, twirling her braided hair with her finger. "I can't wait to go hunting next year!"

"Whoa—You want to hunt too? This is a guys' trip."

I know Molly's a tomboy, always following me around, asking to come fishing and catching frogs, but this is pushing it.

"Tater!" Dad said in a stern voice. "Molly's welcome to come hunting next year when she's old enough. This is a family trip..." Placing his hands on the table, he leaned

31

forward, looking me in the eye as if pronouncing an irreversible edict.

I glared at Molly, tightening my mouth and narrowing my eyes. Last thing I needed was my sister ruining everything with complaining, or even worse, showing me up.

"I hope you don't get one this year!" Molly said, sticking her tongue out and kicking me in the shin under the table.

"Hey, that hurt! What'd you do that for?"

"Now, now, let's simmer down," Mom said. "We're a family, and just because we're a family doesn't mean we're always going to agree. Let's work together and pull through."

"Well... If she can come, then Bandit should be able to come too!" I said, folding my arms.

"Let it go, Tate," Dad said firmly. "She has as much right to come as you do. You know very well dogs are not for deer hunting."

After supper, it was my turn for dish duty. I always hated it, but had long since given up on complaining, knowing if I did, I would get the lecture about not doing my part and needing to pitch in.

After the cleanup was complete, we all sat down and listened to Dad read. He did this often at night, and depending on the book, I quite enjoyed it. Sounds of chirping crickets filled the night air as a cool breeze blew through the open window.

Bandit seemed to like the stories as well, lying by my side on the family room floor as images of Old Dan and Little Ann romping through the forest, trailing coons, and barking up trees filled our minds.

I wished he and I could hunt more together. He wasn't a bad pheasant dog, but there wasn't much coon hunting in my neck of the woods. And by himself, he was no match for a mountain lion.

Later that night, as I lay in bed, my mind swirled with images of the white Ghost Deer bounding through the forest, his massive rack of antlers like a crown on his head. *I have to find him again. I just have to,* I thought, just before I drifted off to sleep.

CHAPTER 5

THE HUNT BEGINS

SAWTOOTH MOUNTAINS, BASE CAMP

AUGUST 30th, 1987, 4:35 AM

As I stepped from the camp trailer, my breath frosted in the crisp, pine-scented air, rising in the early morning lantern light. The stars looked like distant fires filling the blackened sky. A couple of months had passed since my last run-in with the Bogsleys. The opening day of the bow hunt had finally arrived.

I reflected on the day before. By the time we'd loaded up our supplies, hauled up the trailer, and set up camp, we had settled in just before dark.

And here it is, dark still, I thought. *Sure feels like the same day… Boy am I tired.* I stretched, attempting to work out the kinks from a night filled with excited imaginations of bounding deer, twirling arrows, and very little sleep.

Sounds of plastic dragging on metal broke the silence as Dad loaded our bows and equipment into the back of the brown 1966 Ford pickup. The truck had been in the family since what seemed like the dawn of creation and was a regular part of the crew.

"Hop on in, Tater," Dad called. "Time to get going." Decked out in camouflage, it was difficult to see his tall outline blending into the shadows, but I could tell he was waving me over.

Grandpa came alongside, giving me a wink and a nudge as he motioned towards the middle bench seat. We climbed in and shut the creaking doors.

Dad started up the engine, and it awakened with a roar. He shifted the pickup into gear and we were off for the hunting adventure of a lifetime.

Amidst the familiar sounds of the humming motor and rattling doors, I asked the question that had been plaguing my sleep every night for the past two months.

"Will we see him again, Dad?"

"See who, son?"

"You know... the Ghost Deer!"

He chuckled, looked over at Grandpa, and cleared his throat. "Tate—I'm not sure. We're in the right area, but deer like that aren't spotted very often. You were lucky to see him at all."

"But why?" I asked. "He's got to be in the same place." I knew full well of Dad's concerns. I just didn't want to admit it. We'd scouted that same location several times since sighting the white buck without a lick of luck.

Grandpa turned to face me, a warm smile stretched across his face. He stroked his gray mustache and then folded his arms across his belly, turning back to watch the road. "Tater, when I was your age, I saw a big buck like the one you've been talking about. He wasn't white, but he had a very large rack."

"The King, Grandpa?"

"Yes, that's the one, and boy, was he something!"

"Did anyone ever tag him?"

"No, I don't believe they did. Over the years, I heard of occasional sightings. I'm guessing he died of old age on a mountain peak somewhere."

I imagined The King bounding through the thick subalpine firs atop a towering ridgeline, working his way around boulders and fallen rock. The mighty buck's ears perked back on alert as he scanned for danger, his massive rack of antlers turning from side to side. Steam poured from the buck's nostrils, igniting the cold air. The Old Muley slowed to a strut, climbing like royalty towards a lone mountain peak.

Voices brought me back from my enchanted dreams.

"Hey Tater—Tate!"

"Uh, yeah Dad?"

"So, where do you think he's hiding?"

"Well—I guess I don't know. Do you reckon he's in the ravine where I saw him last?"

"I'm not sure, bud; I suppose he's moved higher into the range by now."

Grandpa cleared his throat. "Rod, do you remember the road leading to that upper mountain basin?"

"Which one?" Dad asked.

"Up Sawtooth Mountain, you know—the area I call Razorback Ridge."

"Yeah, I remember. Isn't that where we saw those two big bucks years back?"

"That's the one. I told Sam we would head there. He and the boys will join us back at camp tonight."

"Does he know where we're camping?" Dad questioned.

"I talked to him the other day. He shouldn't have a hard time finding us."

"Sounds great!" Dad said.

"Once we get there, we can cut over to the end of the basin—up top, where the cliffs are."

Dad downshifted as we climbed. "That works for me."

Grandpa scratched at the stubble on his chin and motioned towards the north. "There are plenty of thick pines for a big buck to hide, and good water and food sources. Few people even know the area exists. The road's long since been overgrown."

"Now, as the crow flies, isn't the basin just a few miles above the ravine where Tater saw the Ghost Deer?" Dad asked.

Grandpa smiled. "Yes, now that you mention it, I believe it is. What are your thoughts, Tater?"

"I'm in!" I said. "I haven't been able to stop thinking about Old Muley since I saw him."

Dad smiled and slapped his knee. "Well, it's settled then; Razorback Ridge it is!"

CHAPTER 6
MOUNTAIN FORTRESS

It was still early and very dark out. The rhythmic rattles of the old truck soon lulled my heavy eyes to sleep. I awoke to see Dad turning left onto a forgotten road, apparent by the tall grass and occasional sagebrush growing on it. The engine roared as he downshifted, preparing for the climb. From there, we cut back and forth, climbing switchbacks up the mountain.

A light glow appeared above the ridgeline—sunrise was close. In the darkness, the surrounding trees appeared as giant, majestic shadows. Thick lodgepole pines lined the road, along with occasional aspens and brush-filled meadows.

Near the top, the road dropped into a large bowl-shaped valley filled with subalpine firs and large jutting rocks. After a time, the trees thinned, expanding into a wide basin surrounded by towering cliffs, like the walls of a grand fortress.

Could they be protecting the Ghost Deer? I wondered.

The road soon faded, disappearing into a grassy meadow about a mile from the cliffs. The truck came to a stop as the dusty brakes screeched in protest of the journey's end.

"We're here!" Dad said. "Now, let's unload our gear and see if we can find that old Ghost Deer."

My hands shook with bottled excitement as images of a large buck with massive antlers filled my mind. Once Grandpa climbed out, I bailed out of the truck so fast you would have thought there was a skunk in the cab.

Unpacking our bows, we strapped on our backpacks filled with supplies. It was still dark when we began hiking, but light enough that we no longer needed a flashlight.

Silence permeated the forest as we worked our way towards the base of the castle-like cliffs, the only sounds our rhythmic breathing and the sagebrush sliding against our pant legs.

We made good time, with only a mild incline providing resistance. As we drew near the base of the cliff, we found a well-traveled game trail, littered with hoof prints and signs of deer droppings.

"Is that the Ghost Deer's track?" I asked, pointing.

Dad chuckled, placing his large hand on my shoulder. "No, bud, it's an elk track, could be a smaller bull or a cow. Remember, the Ghost Deer had big tracks, but they flared out on the tips. You know that's a sign of age, right?"

I frowned and kicked at the dirt to cover the tracks.

Dad scooped up a handful of powdered dust from the trail, letting it run through his fingers. As he watched it blow off in the wind, he asked, "Where should we go from here, Dad? The sun'll be up soon; we should hunker down."

Grandpa Silas scanned the hillside, taking a moment to catch his breath. "I can't say where Old Muley's hiding, but if I were him, I would either use the cliffs or the thick pines for shelter and have plenty of escape routes. By the dust you dropped, it looks like the wind's in our favor. Let's head down the trail and find a spot with good cover. If we find a watering hole, all the better."

The morning sky faded from black to a dark blue. We needed to get into position, and quick. It had taken longer than we planned to get up the mountain, and from the tone of their voices, I sensed their urgency.

We soon left the openness of the large basin and entered the trees. Thick pines and quaking aspens surrounded us. After a time, we came to a small meadow with scattered trees and a pond in the far corner. Green moss filled the water, and tall grass grew in the shallows.

Grandpa motioned with his hand. "This looks like the ideal spot," he whispered. "I'll stay here on the downwind side of the meadow by the large pine and watch the trail. Rod, what do you and Tater say about going over and watching the pond? I bet there are some thirsty animals this morning..."

Dad smiled and looked at me, squeezing my shoulder. "Sounds great," he said. "This looks perfect!"

CHAPTER 7
BUCK FEVER

Working our way off the trail, we snuck into the trees along the meadow's edge. As we neared the pond, I saw it wasn't deep, about three feet in the middle. *Darn, no fish,* I thought. *Would've been nice to do some bow fishing if the deer hunting doesn't pan out.*

I tugged on Dad's arm. "Can we go look for tracks?"

"Better not, bud. It would leave our scent. Let's just hope they come in this morning and take a drink." Pointing to a large fallen tree, he said, "We can hide over there. It's got excellent cover and a clear view of the water."

Once in position, we took off our packs and sat in the tall grass. Within moments, I sprang up, patting my rear end. "Wet!" I hissed, scanning the ground. Cold dampness seeped into my pant legs as I examined the droplets of morning dew covering the nearby blades.

Dad nudged me, whispering, "Tater, pull out an arrow."

I pulled a long shaft with green and yellow fletchings from my quiver. *Yep, this is the one,* I thought, admiring the four steel blades in the morning light.

Dad gave me another nudge. "Hurry, bud!"

I nodded and nocked the arrow on my bow. I took off my camouflaged hat and ran my fingers through tangled hair, repositioning myself next to the fallen tree.

"Dad, when are the deer coming?" I asked.

"Be patient, Tater, it takes time."

A few minutes later, I whispered, "Dad... it's been a while. Are we in the right place?"

After a few more rounds of questions, he gave me a pat on the shoulder and stood, motioning to a spot in the brush twenty feet back. I got up to follow, but he held out his hand. Plopping back down, I crossed my legs and sighed as he moved over.

Waiting for the fish to take my bait is hard, but man, oh man, this is harder.

I broke a small twig with my fingers, throwing it to the side.

The morning sun streamed through the trees as golden ribbons filtered through the branches. Dew-filled brush sparkled in the meadow. This same forest of quiet darkness had become a land of magic and wonder.

My stomach growled. A chipmunk scurried up a tree nearby. His little tail twitched as he sat on a thin branch, chewing on some sort of seed, holding it with both hands. *Might have found a pine nut,* I thought. *I wonder if he'd share.*

Squirrels chattered in the distant pines and birds chirped their favorite morning melody. I sucked in the cool air—laced with smells of pine and damp wood. *Ah yes... a perfect morning in the mountains—to be hunting—even better.* I smiled at this thought and exhaled slowly, grateful for the day.

Something rustled in the brush behind me, drawing my mind back to the hunt. The noise was close. I didn't dare move my head or blink an eye, freezing with a mixture of excitement and fear. I strained to hear each detail, every sense enhanced. *What's behind me?* I questioned.

I wondered what Dad was doing about the situation. *Only silence in his direction...*

The dogwood bush rustled again.

Could it be a deer?

A light padding noise sounded as something ran across a log.

That's strange...

A chill rippled along my spine, questions flooding my thoughts.

Is it a bobcat? Maybe a mountain lion or a wolf? The footsteps sure don't sound like a deer.

What I heard next made the hair on the back of my neck stand up and salute, almost popping my camouflaged hat right off. Something was trying to open the zipper of my backpack!

The tether tied to my zipper was getting yanked back and forth! Commotion broke out, filled with high-pitched screeching.

Whirling around, I turned to face certain death. My mouth dropped and my eyes shot open with unbelief. Right behind me, sitting on my backpack, were two fluff-tail

47

squirrels, each with arms wrapped around my Snickers bar poking out from the zipper pocket. Those little rascals were attempting to rob me of my prized treat!

Scrambling and screeching, the squirrels broke into commotion, legs spinning as they tried to escape. Their problem was, neither one would let go. They started running in a circle, hugging the candy bar as if it were a rigid pole sticking out of the ground, one on each side.

Faster and faster, they raced until they became nothing more than flashes of brown-and-white fur and loud chattering. I went to brush the thieving creatures off but pulled back.

The last thing I need is a case of the rabies to end my hunt.

Finally, one of them fell off the bar, tumbling to the ground, squalling, and throwing a fit—madder than a nest of bug-eyed hornets. The off-centered effect gave the other squirrel the leverage he needed to yank my Snickers from the zipper and roll down the pack to the forest floor.

Instantly, he dragged my treat away through the pine needles and scattered twigs at lightning speed. I dove for him but only got a handful of moss-covered branches and a mouthful of rancid dirt, which I spit out like poison.

Pushing myself up, I yanked out a rock and threw it at the scoundrel, just missing him as he scurried over a log. Then, jumping to my feet, I ran after him.

"You little thief!" I yelled.

It was no use. Within seconds, he had beaten me.

Dad busted out laughing, throwing all hunting protocol to the wind. "The funniest thing I ever saw!" he said, slapping his leg.

I threw a branch in the squirrel's direction and glared at Dad. "Glad you think it's funny!"

Grandpa stood up, his arms spread wide, looking confused by all the commotion. Yet, from his smile, I figured his imagination was filling him in.

"It's alright, Tater, you can have mine," Dad said.
I huffed out a sigh. "No, I'll be fine." Chuckling, I said, "I wish I'd eaten it in the truck on the way up, like I'd wanted to."

"Looks like we'll have to get us some squirrel-proof zippers," Dad said, smiling.

I laughed. "Guess so... And to think I was worried about the bears. Who would have thought?"

Dad scratched at his ear, scanning the area. "Well— Tater, we better hunker down and try to regroup. With all the noise we've made, we won't be seeing anything for a while."

"Ok..." I huffed. "More waiting," I mumbled, plopping onto the ground.

Time passed and the morning sun felt comforting, my hands and feet no longer tingly with stinging pain. My pants were drier than before, yet still cold to the touch.

Grandpa appeared to watch the trail, but with his back to the tree and his hat over his eyes, and I questioned his motives. My mind soon drifted into daydreams of the Ghost Deer. *Would I ever see him again?*

Reed's words flashed through my mind for the hundredth time. *'Now, why don't you tell us where to find him? We'll take care of him for you, nice and tidy like.'*

On the way up, I saw a rusted-out two-tone Chevy truck parked off the side in the darkness. I knew Reed was driving age, but I rarely saw him behind the wheel. I doubted they had any running vehicle parked in that junk pile of a yard of theirs.

It had been almost two months since I'd seen the Bogsleys, which was odd. After my last run-in with them, I told Mom I broke my bike—I hadn't wanted her to worry. I felt horrible as I remembered this lie. Despite my guilt, I kept asking for rides to my grandparents', making excuses for why I hadn't fixed the chain. I was grateful for her patience. Yet, from her narrowed eyes and folded arms, I could tell she knew I wasn't being honest.

I scooped up a handful of moist dirt, letting it trickle through my fingers. "When I get back—I'll make it right," I whispered, tossing it on the ground.

If the Bogsleys found the buck, they would use any means necessary to get him, and that bothered me. *Are they following us... or are my fears just feeding me lies?* I considered this thought. Whatever the answer—the weight of the bet played heavy on my mind.

I leaned back, settling against a log, listening to the rustling leaves overhead.

I then picked up a broken branch and drew a buck with big antlers in the dirt. *"I wish,"* I whispered. Brushing it away with my hand, I drew an elk, a bear, then a beaver. I chuckled. *Not much of a beaver... looks like a rat with a frying pan for a tail.*

A big black stink bug came waddling out of a patch of grass. I reached towards it, preparing to flick it away. Suddenly, there was a loud *"thump—thump, crack!"* The noise came from the trees to my left.

Ducking, I reached over and picked up my bow. Rising to my knees, I scanned the forest—*nothing!* Another loud *"crack!"* sounded, this time closer. *It might be a deer, likely several,* I thought, fidgeting with excitement.

Grateful we still had the wind to our advantage, I waited. As they neared, glimpses of brown fur passed through the trees. Dad motioned for me to get ready. Sounds of breaking branches and thumping hooves increased as I struggled to control my breathing and gripped my bow tight. Several deer passed as I crouched behind a nearby bush.

Doe, fawn... doe, doe, buck!

I fought against my shaking hands, snatching an arrow from the quiver. A large three-point stepped out, his head and antlers visible. He looked around, sniffed the air, and put his head down to graze.

The buck raised his head, looking in the opposite direction, flicking his ears at swarming flies. I drew back my bow from a kneeling position and carefully stood, leveling on him with my 20-yard sight pin, concealed by the vegetation in front of me. He glanced in my direction, chewing on a small branch hanging from the side of his mouth. I froze, wondering if he would see me.

The tautness of the bowstring's pull pressed into my fingers, burning as I fought against the tension. *Just a few more seconds. Hold it—come on, come on now... Just a little farther...*

The three-point stepped forward, his head, neck and front quarters now exposed.

It's now or never.

I let the arrow slip from my fingers and heard the sharp twang of the bowstring. The buck lunged as my arrow blazed through the air with lightning speed.

Just before it hit its mark—a tree branch deflected the arrow, driving it into the dirt!

"Dang it!"

Ears cocked back, the buck bolted. His head and antlers bounced up and down through the tall brush, and in seconds he disappeared into the trees.

From there, it just got worse. Unknown to me, the blasted three-point was not alone. About ten yards behind, hidden by a fallen pine tree, was a big four-point buck. As I reached for another arrow, he turned, bounding into the cover of the trees, leaving me nothing but glimpses of white rump and bobbing antlers.

"Ahhhh! I had him, Dad!"

"I thought so too, bud."

I threw my bow onto the ground. "Darn branch—got in the way!"

Dad straightened, and his face tightened as he folded his arms. "Tate, get your bow! That's no way to act when you don't get what you want!"

"At home, I nailed the target every time!"

"It's hard alright, but that's what makes it worth it."

"What's all the fuss about?" Grandpa asked, coming up from behind. He grinned, slapping me on the shoulder. "It looks like you got a shot!"

"Yeah... but I missed him."

"It's alright, you're not the first—won't be the last either."

I told Grandpa the entire story and filled him in on the details of the squirrel situation.

He chuckled. "I wondered what was going on over here. Something sure was making a racket." Smiling, he nudged me on the arm. "Thought you were holding out for Old Muley?"

"When I saw those antlers, I just couldn't take it, Grandpa! I had to shoot!"

He chuckled. "I know the feeling. Now let's get your arrow."

We found my arrow. Just as I figured, only small slivers of bark, no signs of hitting anything but a tree. "So, what should we do now?" I asked, brushing off the dirt from the tip.

"Well…" Dad said, "It's getting later, and with all the commotion, I'm guessing we've run out our luck. I'd say let's have a snack and hit the trail. Let's see what we can find."

He turned to Grandpa. "How does that sound?"

"Good to me," he replied. "How about you, Tater?"

"Yep, I'm in. Let's do some exploring. I'm done with this spot! I've had nothing but trouble."

CHAPTER 8
THE RACE

We loaded our packs and hit the trail, following the cliff deeper into the forest. After a time, the towering rock wall became shorter until it faded away into a meadow. Turning, we worked our way into a small canyon along the back of the cliff.

The trail was steep and slow going. Upon reaching the bottom, I took off my jacket as we stopped for a break. We pulled out our sandwiches and mulled over plans for the evening hunt. As we did, Grandpa Silas started telling us about some of his adventures when he was a kid.

"I had Bobby Darnell hot on my tail. I could hear his feet pounding and the brush crunching right behind me," he said, making a running motion with his arms. "It was dark, no moon in sight, but I had a hunch where they'd hid their flag, and I was dead set on getting it.

"Problem was, I could hardly see a lick besides the dark shapes of the trees and the sagebrush. So, when I saw an opening to the right, and it looked like a clear path, I took it.

"Suddenly, the ground disappeared! My feet and arms were spinning through the air, and all I saw was the stars up in the sky mixed with patches of blackness," he said, twirling his arms around. "I landed hard, and I could feel pain prickling all through my back and legs."

"What happened next?" I asked, leaning forward.

"Well—when I woke up, Bobby was kneeling over me, shaking my arm and asking if I was dead."

"Were you?"

He laughed hard, holding his belly. "I sure hope not," he said, patting his chest with both hands. "With how bad I hurt, I thought I was dying—but I got through it alright."

"You fell off a cliff, then?"

He chuckled. "No, just into the gravel pit up there in the foothills above town. Learned to be more careful playing night games after that."

*   *   *

A short time later, a cottontail rabbit bounced out below, unaware of our presence. I took a small carrot out of my lunch sack and rolled it down the hill in his direction. To my disappointment, the carrot startled him, causing him to run off.

After a few minutes, the rabbit's gray ears poked through the grass as his head tilted back, sniffing for the carrot. Soon he hopped out, nudged it with his nose, and started munching. About halfway through, his head jerked up as his big black eyes blinked in our direction.

Interesting. He's just staring at me, unafraid.

He blinked his eyes again, turned, and bounced into the bushes.

After lunch, we continued down the ravine, along the backside of the cliff, soon coming out of the thick pines into a small meadow. The deer trail we were following disappeared, forcing us to blaze our own path through the tall grass and underbrush. As we neared the other side of the meadow, a loud snort froze us in our tracks.

About fifteen yards away, a cow moose and her calf stood up in a patch of scrub oak, apparently startled by our presence.

The mama moose sniffed the air, staring us down with her large black eyes. She let out another loud snort, shaking her head and pawing clumps of sod from the ground with her front hooves.

I remembered hearing somewhere that there was nothing more dangerous than a mother defending her young, and I was pretty sure we were the ones she was preparing to defend against.

I looked back and nudged Dad. His gaze was fixed on the moose like a fly stuck to a honey jar.

I whispered, "What should we do?"

There was no need for a response. The mama moose let out a roar, dipping her head and kicking up dirt and grass as she charged.

"Run!" Dad yelled.

He hooked his arm around my back and gave me a turbo boost down the hill, propelling me forward so fast my feet nearly burst into flames. The race was on!

Now, I had not seen Grandpa run for some years, and I wasn't sure if he was up for it, but he surprised me.

As the pounding hooves and breaking brush neared, not only was the hair on my neck standing up, but I think I grew hair on my ears as well.

To any onlooker, it would have appeared that we had a grizzly bear breathing down our necks, and a fat, juicy steak strapped to our backs.

Through the trees we ran, breaking branches and dodging brush like a world-record Olympic hurdling team.

My heart pounded like the hooves of a racehorse as the entire forest seemed to claw at me with fury.

Not long into the race for our lives, I tripped on a clump of grass, which launched me into the air like an astronaut going into orbit. The world spun—once, twice, and then I crashed into a large patch of brush, face-planting into the dirt.

Mom had always told me to floss, but getting twigs up my nose and grass stuck in my teeth was not my idea of a good time.

As I lay there tangled sideways in the stabbing branches with my face pressed onto the sod below, I was not ranking my first hunt very high on the scale of legend.

The moose! Where's the moose?

I scrambled from the brush, tearing the sleeve of my camo shirt.

Dad and Grandpa caught up, towering over me as I kneeled on the ground and gasped for air.

Through sporadic rasping breaths, Dad said, "Are you... are you okay... bud?"

"Yeah, I guess so."

"She's… She's stopped… not following…. Not following anymore," Dad panted out.

Dad pulled me up, dusting me off. "Tater, you sure you're okay?"

I smiled half-heartedly and said, "I'm okay, just a little dirty and scratched up." I took off my hat and swatted at my camouflage shirt, which at this point had a lot more nature on it than I recalled.

"Dang brush, tearing my camo!" I said, examining my sleeve. "Wow, that was close! I thought I was going to die!"

"I figure God was looking out for us today, Tater," Dad said, dusting off my back.

"Yeah, I reckon so… Are you okay, Grandpa?" I asked.

Bent over, with his hands on his knees, my granddad wheezed, his asthma taking a toll.

"I'm alright, Tater… Just give me a minute… I'll be alright."

"It looks like you lost your hat, Gramps."

He smiled, wiping sweat from his forehead and combing his fingers through jumbled gray hair. "Looks like I did. Hit a branch back there, near took my head off."

After Grandpa caught his breath, with some caution, we went back and found his camo hat hanging on a tree. The funny thing is a darn squirrel had already curled up inside.

I slowly lifted the hat from the tree and whispered, "That didn't take long. Looks like you're going to have to fight a squirrel for your hat, Gramps."

He chuckled.

Suddenly, the squirrel opened his eyes so wide they about bugged out of his head. In an instant, he jumped out of the hat, with his feet spinning in the air. As he hit the ground, he darted off, jumping and chattering like we'd stolen his favorite nut.

Dad laughed, "Looks like we're not the only ones running for our lives around here."

Grandpa picked up his hat, examining it for holes and checking to see if the fluff-tailed furball had left any presents in it. He slapped it back on his head and stroked his mustache. "Well—since that's taken care of, where should we go now?"

"I don't know—I just want to find the Ghost Deer," I said. "In fact, I'd settle for anything sporting antlers."

Grandpa chuckled. "Got the old buck fever, do ya?" he asked, giving me a wink that marked both my excitement and his knowledge of my bet with the Bogsleys.

"Yeah—I guess so. This isn't as easy as I thought."

"I reckon not," he said, placing his arm on my shoulder. "Hang in there, Tater. It'll work out." He smiled and waved towards a patch of trees. "Hey, how about we cut through those thick pines? If we're quiet, we might just catch a bedded buck."

"Sure, why not," I said. "Old Muley's going to be hiding out deep. The thicker, the better."

CHAPTER 9
THE WHITE BUCK

As we entered the towering trees, the forest darkened. With no trails, we picked our way through the maze of fallen logs and dense branches. I soon realized that 'thicker the better' was a bad idea.

A buck will run circles around us in here.

In the distance, a branch broke and a squirrel chattered.

"See, there goes one now," I whispered.

"What's that, Tate?" Dad asked.

"Ah, nothing..."

We've got to get out of here, I thought, shaking my head. *There won't be a buck left. May as well be honking a horn.*

Wiping sweat from his eyes, Dad nodded, as if reading my mind.

After a time, we broke free of the dense forest, cut across a small meadow, and headed up a hill. Maneuvering around several large boulders, we came to a ridgeline.

Dad took his handkerchief from his pocket and wiped his forehead. "Tater, will you go check it out?" he asked, pointing to the ridge. "Let us know what's on the other side. Grandpa and I will wait here in the shade and catch our breath."

"Sure."

I cut around a scrub oak and crept to the edge of the ridge. A meadow with scattered trees extended sixty yards before dropping down a steep hill. My bow sifted through the grass, tickling my fingers as I crept forward. Reaching the edge, I kneeled.

To my left, a hill covered with juniper trees blocked my view. On my right, a glistening river lined with thick willows snaked through a long meadow below, filled with grass and scattered aspens.

I glassed the area with my binoculars, searching the trees and thick brush, straining to see a flick of an ear or a twitch of a tail. After a few minutes, a patch of gray, jumbled branches came into view by the river's edge, lying against what looked like a thick, white log.

High water must have piled them up, I thought.

Tiring of my search, I lowered my binoculars, wondering if there were any beaver in the area. It was a perfect spot for them.

As I gazed into the distance, movement caught my eye. *Did that branch pile just move?* I fumbled for my binoculars and dropped them into the grass. "No...can't be..." I whispered, as I snatched them up, pressing my face against the round lenses magnifying my view.

The gnarled clump of branches shifted again! A white snout was now poking out from the front of it, drinking water.

Two long ears and a thick neck extended back to a white body, carved with bulging muscles.

"Holy cow!" I said, shaking my head and lowering my binoculars.

Although he was 500 yards away, now that I had him spotted, I could still see the mass of antlers belonging to the most monstrous buck I'd ever dreamed of.

Grass rustled from behind as Dad came and kneeled beside me. "You okay, bud?" he whispered.

"Why?" I asked, shaking my head and rubbing my eyes.

"Well... you're acting kind of funny."

"I... I think I'm seeing the Ghost Deer," I said. "Either that, or I hit my head too hard when the moose about ran us over."

"The Ghost Deer?" Grandpa asked. "Where?"

I pointed. "Right there. Can't you see him?"

"No."

"In the willows—down by the river."

Dad held up a hand, shielding his eyes from the sun.

"Where now?"

"Right there!" I said, shaking my pointed finger.

"Holy smokes, unbelievable!"

Grandpa chimed in. "You're not hallucinating, he's real alright!"

"Let's use those juniper trees over there to get a closer look," Dad said, pointing. With a motion of his hand, he beckoned me to follow.

I crawled through the tall dusty grass, my palms pricking against the stubble. My nose tickled as it rubbed against the dirt covered blades, forcing me to sneeze. I quickly buried my face deep into my jacket, attempting to muffle the sound. *Shoot! I hope that didn't ruin it,* I thought, kicking myself inside.

As we neared the trees, my heart raced with anticipation. Crouching, we used the cover of the junipers until we reached the edge.

I got down on my stomach and peered through the tall grass at the crest of the hill, which dropped to the river below. To my left, a small waterfall cascaded down the rocks into a shallow pool of clear water, feeding the stream I had seen earlier.

Approximately 400 yards away, Old Muley drank from the pool. Massive as an elk, his thick neck and broad shoulders held a rack of antlers that resembled two tree branches on each side, filled with more points than I could count.

Dad pulled out his high-power spotting scope and gasped. "Oh boy! I've never seen anything like him."

"Can I see, Dad?"

"Sure, bud."

After a look, I lowered the scope and shook my head, attempting to clear my vision. The Ghost Deer was in plain sight, not a figment of my imagination as the Bogsleys had accused.

I'll show them! They'll have to leave me alone forever when I get this buck. I'll have bragging rights for years.

I couldn't quite put my finger on it, but there was much more to him than antlers, white fur, and a powerful build. A king of grand proportion sipped the water below.

Grandpa gazed through his binoculars as he examined the buck. He smiled, shaking his head. "I feel like I'm seeing The King again," he said. "This brings back many memories.

You know, Tater, this buck is much older and larger than The King was. I never thought I would see the day!"

"Is he the same buck, Gramps?"

"I don't see how. I was just a boy then. Same area, but I'm sure The King has long since passed away."

Dad nudged me and whispered. "Look, the old boy has his head up, sniffing the air."

"What do you reckon he's going to do?" I asked.

"Looks like he senses danger."

"Does he smell us?"

"Not sure. We're still quite far away."

Grandpa pulled up a dead blade of grass and peeled off a thin piece, letting it drop. The sliver twirled through the air, floating down the hill towards the buck.

"Oh, no…!" Dad said. "He's going to smell us."

Grandpa pointed. "Looks like he already has."

I looked to see every hunter's worst nightmare. The Ghost Deer had our location pegged. Despite our camouflage and hidden position, he glared up at us. Dad's jaw gaped open—so close to the ground ants could have done pullups from his whiskers.

The buck shook his head and massive rack as if calling out a challenge. Then, digging into the ground with his front hooves, he snorted. The sound echoed through the canyon and surrounding cliffs, daring us to come closer.

He dipped his head and spun around, smashing his rack through the dead branches of a fallen tree at the edge of the river. The buck splintered them as he ripped through, splattering remnants of wood and bark onto the nearby brush. He scowled in our direction, snorted, and raised up on his hind legs, pounding his hooves into the water, spraying droplets across the pool.

I pressed deeper into the grass, attempting to remain out of sight.

"It's okay, bud," Dad said.

The Ghost Deer waited, as if calling for a response to his challenge. Snorting, he shook his bush-like rack again. Then, lunging forward, he strutted into the shallow pool, only his body exposed now.

"What's he doing?" I asked.

Dad rubbed the stubble on his face. "Maybe he's thirsty."

"Look," Grandpa said, pointing. "He's going in!"

"What? Can't be…" Dad whispered.

The Ghost Deer turned, dipped his head low and lumbered through the pool towards the waterfall. White droplets sprayed off his back as he entered the pounding water, and within seconds, he was gone.

I shot up. "No! Not now!"

"Let's go!" Dad said, bolting up from the ground, waving for us to follow. "We've got to get down there!"

I scrambled to my feet and trailed behind Dad, already half leaping and half sliding down the hill, my mind racing with possibilities.

CHAPTER 10
SECRET LAIR

The hill was steep and difficult, costing us several valuable minutes. Upon reaching the base, we headed towards the river through a sea of tall grass and scattered willows filling the ravine.

The problem was, Old Muley's tracks littered the damp bank on the other side of the pool. The waterfall cascading down the cliff, covered with green moss and vegetation, posed quite an obstacle. That, and the river it fed, formed a fine fence line for those of us valuing dry feet and britches.

Cool mist rose from the pounding water, soothing my sweat-beaded forehead and making it impossible to see through the veil of white water.

"Did he really go in?" I asked.

Dad squinted in the sunlight, probing for an entry. "It sure looked like he went in. However, from our angle, he may have just walked behind, climbing the hill by that patch of pines over there." He scratched the stubble on his cheek and chuckled. "Tater, this old buck you've found sure has me questioning my sanity. My eyes tell me he did, but my brain tells me I'm crazy."

Grandpa slapped Dad's back, a big jolly grin planted on his face. "Now let's stop all this yarn spinning," he said. "There's only one way to find out, and standing here talking about it won't bring Old Muley home."

"What should we do?" I asked.

He looked around, searching for something. Then, pointing to the ground, he said, "Tater, grab that big rock over there."

"This one?"

"Yeah, that'll work."

I dug the large rock out of the mud, hefting it waist high, forgetting to breathe. Like a hidden iceberg, it was larger than it looked. Yet, too proud to ask for help, I strained under its weight, feeling like a bug-eyed frog as I waddled back.

"Bigger than I realized," Grandpa said, chuckling. "Good, now hand it to your dad and let him try out his old pitching arm. Rod… throw it at the waterfall."

"What?"

"Yeah, let's see if it goes in," Grandpa said, putting his hands on his knees as if preparing for a show.

Dad looked at the rock, and then back at Grandpa, giving me a hard glance as if to say, *I wish you'd gotten a smaller one*, taking it with both hands.

"Alright, stand back…" Dad said. Pausing, he nodded to my compound bow. "It may be a good idea to grab an arrow and get it drawn, in case Old Muley pays us a visit."

I nocked an arrow and pulled back, placing the bowstring against my cheek.

"Okay, ready!" I said. "Let her rip!"

The way Dad reared back and staggered forward, whirling around, you would have thought he was trying to be the next Scottish log-throwing champion. Regardless, the rock hurled through the air, right into the center of the waterfall. As soon as it hit, the pounding water swept it down into the pool.

A few seconds of silence passed.

"Well—where is he?" I questioned.

"Huh," Grandpa said. "It didn't go in like I figured. I was hoping it would either stir out Old Muley or give us a clue about what was on the other side—sorry, Rod."

"No worries," Dad said, rubbing his shoulder.

Our options were fading like a puddle of evaporating water. The Ghost Deer had outsmarted us like a fox with many holes.

Dad walked over and gripped my shoulder softly. He sighed heavily. "Well, Tater, what do you say? Should we give up on the old buck and work our way downriver?"

"No, Dad! We can't quit. Not after being this close."

"Well, what should we do then? It seems like we're at a dead end."

What can I do? I thought, as my hopes broke into a million pieces.

Then it hit me! *Why hadn't I realized this before?* "Hey Dad, I have an old blunt-tipped arrow here in my quiver, you know, the one I use for practice on dirt clumps?"

"Yeah..."

"Well—why don't I shoot this arrow at the waterfall? It'll be fast enough to either make it through or bounce off the rocks. How about it?"

He chuckled and smiled. "That's a great idea! I guess you're right. We couldn't live with ourselves if we didn't answer this mystery."

"Yes!" I said as I leaped high into the air and tugged at my quiver, anxiously struggling to pull the blunt free. I drew back and looked at Grandpa, who was grinning ear to ear. He gave me a nod.

Right into the waterfall the arrow went—and I mean right in, no bounce and no arrow sticking out, nothing.

"Whoopee!" I yelled.

"Let's go in!" I said, jumping up and swinging my fist in the air with victory. "He's in there alright! Let's go get him!"

Dad held up his hands. "Whoa, tiger! You can't just go strutting up to a waterfall, knock on the door, and invite yourself in."

"Why not? The Ghost Deer did it. Why can't we?"

Now I'm not sure if Dad didn't think we could do it, or just didn't want to get wet behind the ears. But he sure seemed to hem and haw about it.

Grandpa came to my defense. "Well, we do have the rain gear in our packs. Except for some wet feet and pant legs, my guess is we'll somehow survive."

Dad laughed at Grandpa's sarcasm. After all, the waterfall was not overpowering, and Grandpa had flat out called his bluff on the getting wet part. Dad smiled and put his hand on my shoulder. "Well, Tater, it looks like I'm outnumbered. I guess I need a good bath today after all."

Grandpa waved his hand in front of his nose and laughed. "You've got that right! You're making my nose hairs curl. A bath might do you some good."

Dad chuckled. "Well then, let's go have us a shower."

We unloaded our rain gear and suited up. Dad volunteered to go first, just in case the experiment went down bad and we had to wave the flag of retreat.

With his backpack strapped under his black-hooded rain poncho and the bow gripped in his left hand, Dad looked like the Hunchback of Notre Dame, the emperor on *Star Wars*, and Robin Hood, all rolled up in one.

"We're in fine hands," I said, glancing over at Grandpa.

He nodded.

Dad stepped into the pool. "Whoa, this is cold!" he protested.

Grandpa laughed. "You're committed now," he jeered.

Dad's eyebrows furrowed. "How did you guys get me into this?" Sighing, he turned, trudging deeper into the pool.

"It's filling my boots!"

"Ah, quit your bellyaching," Grandpa poked.

"Oh, you'll find out soon enough," Dad fired back.

Within moments, the water came partway up his leg as waves splashed onto his thigh. Nearing the pounding water, Dad looked back at me. "Hey Tate, why don't you throw me a long stick so I can feel out the opening?"

"I shot my arrow right there," I said, pointing.

"I know that…" He waved his arm towards the waterfall. "Need to be certain; running into rock with water pounding on my head isn't something I'll enjoy."

Grandpa chuckled. "You would if you were a big-horned sheep with gills."

"Ah… just get me that stick, will ya, and hurry! My feet feel like ice blocks swallowed them."

"How big?" I asked.

"Just long enough so I can check it out."

I ran along the river and found a large aspen tree, long since fallen. I kicked off a branch and raced back. Breathing hard, I held it out. "Here you go!"

"Just throw it."

It splashed as it struck, spraying him.

"Hey!" he called out. "I know I'm going to get wet, but let's not put the cart before the horse." He grabbed the branch and waved it over his head.

Dad poked at the curtain of water with the stick, starting at the outer edge and working across.

"Nothing here."

My hopes sank.

Towards the center he said, "Whoa!" Then he probed around some more. "I found the opening! It's about five feet wide and six feet tall."

I'd always believed Dad was fearless, yet by the way he dragged this out, you would have thought he was heading into the mouth of a mountain lion.

Hesitating, he yelled back over the pounding water, "Here I go!"

With the stick in front, Dad hunched over and shuffled forward. The water broke over his head and shoulders as he pressed through the waterfall. Within seconds, he disappeared.

"Whoopee!" I yelled. "Can we go in, Grandpa? Can we?"

He smiled at my excitement. "You sure, bud?"

"Of course! Let's go!"

He pointed. "I guess we better. Looks like your dad's inviting us in."

The branch waved back and forth, protruding from the center of the falling water.

We wasted no time plunging into the pool. Thousands of icy needles pricked my feet as we neared the wall of water, my legs tingling with biting pain.

Grandpa motioned for me to come closer.

"You go first," he said. "Grab the stick tight and hold on."

I could hardly see the branch as the splashing water and rolling mist pelted my eyes. Inching forward, I reached out in search of the staff.

I felt like a piece of wood about to be ripped apart by an approaching saw blade as the water stormed down upon the hood of my raincoat.

Latching onto the end of the slippery stick, I wished both hands were free. Yet, not about to let go of my bow, I gave the branch a tug. Dad pulled it forward, guiding me through.

As I ducked low, the water pounded on my head, back and shoulders, roaring in my ears. I stumbled forward, falling against the rock wall. Pain exploded through my face. Scrambling for better footing, I let go of the branch, pushed back, and felt the pressure let up as the crushing water shoved me down. I felt my mind fill with dread as the waterfall drove me under, enveloping me in the biting cold and stealing air from my lungs.

Frantically, I swung my arm through the churning darkness in search of Dad's branch. *Nothing!* I swam, searching along the rock, straining to hold my breath. Crawling along the bottom, I waved my hand through the blackness and felt around for an opening. My lungs burned for need of air.

I have to breathe! I thought, panicking, thrashing through the water in desperation.

A large hand latched onto my arm, pulling me forward. Pain shot through my leg as it collided with something hard. A second later, the hand was gone and I found myself holding onto mud and rock. Gritting my teeth, I crawled forward, dragging my body onto the damp ground.

As I wiped water from my eyes, a blurred image of Dad's smiling face came into view. He pulled me up and wrapped his long arms around me, holding me tight.

"You made it, bud!"

Coughing, I smiled weakly. "Yeah, barely."

"You had me worried!" He pulled my hat from the water, shook it off, and placed it back on my dripping head.

"I thought I was a goner," I said, wrapping my arms around my body, attempting to control my chattering teeth. "I figured the Ghost Deer had won."

"Not yet, but we better get you warmed up," Dad said, removing his jacket. "Here, take this. The flashlight's over by my pack and raincoat." He motioned with his hand. "Scoot on back, so Grandpa has room to get through. I'm sure he's getting cold."

Roots protruded from the dripping rock and dirt above. The surrounding light from the propped-up flashlight faded, leaving darkness beyond.

Preparing to take off my wet jacket and shirt, I bumped my head on the overhead rock. "Ouch!" I said, rubbing it.

"You alright, bud?"

"Yeah, I guess…" I said, gingerly feeling my now-growing goose egg. "Man, this ceiling is low!"

He laughed. "You've got that right!" he said, rubbing his head. "Stay in the middle. You'll have plenty of room."

I backed into the cave, took off my raincoat, and peeled my wet shirt and jacket from my body. My skin prickled with goose bumps, but Dad's dry overcoat was warm and comforting. I rolled up my sleeves with a couple of turns and stuffed the wet clothes in my pack.

Good thing the Bogsleys can't see me in Dad's coat. This looks like a camo dress with pockets, I thought as I examined the draping jacket.

A flickering light shone through the waterfall, appearing as a lighted portal to the outside world. Grandpa's blurred shadow was visible on the other side. I waved at him. "Come on, Gramps, you can do it!"

Dad held the branch through the waterfall, guiding him in. Within seconds, he emerged, hunched over. He wiped the water from his face and shook off his wet hands. "What are you guys getting me into!?" he said with a grin, throwing the raincoat hood back and wiping his dripping face and mustache.

Crowded now in the small entry, I moved back.

Dad called out. "Hey Tater, head into the cave and see what you can find. We'll be right there."

Images flashed through my mind of the Ghost Deer ripping his rack through the fallen tree, shattering the branches.

"You sure, Dad?"

"Yeah—we'll be right there. Just give us a minute to get Grandpa's raincoat off."

Grabbing my flashlight, I crept deeper into the twisting tunnel of rock, listening for even the slightest movement. About twenty feet in, I found my blunt arrow lying on the dirt. In the flashlight's glow, my misty breath rose into the darkness, the damp air smelling musty like roots and wet earth.

Soon, the cave opened into a small cavern. Eager to explore this new world, I shone the flashlight around the open space. The ceiling was close to ten feet, rising to thirty feet at the far wall and extending fifty feet deep.

Piled near the center, a couple of enormous boulders had apparently fallen from a hollowed-out cavity above. *Glad I wasn't here when that happened,* I thought, considering their weight. Several smaller rocks of various shapes and size filled the floor. Water dripped from the ceiling and trickled down the walls like silver snakes, slithering through the cracks in the rock, winding to the floor.

Dad and Grandpa soon came out of the entry tunnel. Grandpa took out his handkerchief to blow his nose, and Dad stretched his back, scanning the walls and ceiling with his flashlight. "Hey, this is great!"

"Sure is," Grandpa agreed.

After taking a few steps, Dad hunched over. "Hey Tate, come on over!" he said, waving his arm. "Boy oh boy, have I got something to show you!"

I ran over.

"What do you see?" he asked, pointing to the light focused on the ground.

"It's the Ghost Deer's track!" I exclaimed, bending down for a closer look.

"Sure is, son," Dad said. "See the flared tips?"

Grandpa pointed. "It's filling with water. That's a fresh one, alright! We better make sure we're ready. With how dark it is, when we get our chance, we won't have much time."

Pausing, he chuckled. "And you better bet he already knows we're here."

Dad cut in, "Hey, what's on the far wall over there?" He pointed the light at what appeared to be a unique coloration of rock.

Grandpa waved his hand, motioning. "Well, let's go have ourselves a look."

We stepped around the rocks littering the floor, passing the boulders in the center of the cavern. As we came closer, I rushed to the cave wall. "Are those petroglyphs, Dad?"

"They sure are! It looks like there's more to this cave than we realized."

We examined the ancient stories carved into the rock.

"How old are they, Dad?"

"Not sure, but from the looks of it, they're Native American, probably hundreds of years old."

"Hey, look over here," Grandpa said, waving us over. "Is this what I think it is?"

"What do you see?" I asked.

"Right here—can't you see it?" His finger focused in on a point of interest to the right. "What would you say these paintings are describing?" he asked.

The image Grandpa pointed at looked like a large white deer with massive antlers. Hunters surrounded the buck. In the next scene, men chased the deer with spears, while others shot arrows. I continued following the images farther along the wall.

"Hey look!" I said, pointing.

The proceeding scenes showed the white buck chasing the hunters as they ran in all directions.

"Is this a painting of the Ghost Deer?" I asked, turning to Grandpa.

He smiled, putting his hand on my shoulder. "It sure looks like a drawing of him. If not, might be a grandfather of his."

I continued examining the wall. From what I could tell, it appeared the ancient artist was depicting clouds with the Ghost Deer walking into them. In the next scene, the hunters kneeled, the buck no longer in the painting.

Dad laughed. "Well, men, it appears we're up against no ordinary buck." He looked at the compound bow he was holding and glanced over at us. "You might even say he's got the upper hand."

CHAPTER 11

UNEXPECTED VISITORS

After a quick break, we pulled out our headlamps and geared up for battle. We followed the buck's tracks to a large triangular crack, eight feet at the base, narrowing to a point twenty feet above our heads.

"Where do you think it goes?" I asked.

A cold droplet of water fell from the rock above, landing on my forehead, tickling my face as it ran down to my nose. The air was damp and musty.

Grandpa came alongside, shining his light into the passageway. "Well, Tater, I don't know, but I can guarantee this—my headlamp's flat out of words."

I looked at him and smiled. He seemed to have a way of putting common sense into any situation.

"Sounds like a good plan," Dad said. "Let's move."

Grandpa pointed out front. "Hey Tater, how about we give you the lead spot?"

"Me?" I asked, looking to Dad for support.

"Yeah, if the big muley's still here, I want you to have the first shot. We'll be ready to back you up."

Was Grandad putting me out as bait for the old buck? I investigated the twisted crack, fading into darkness. *Who even knows what's in there? This is certain death.* Smiling weakly, I nocked an arrow on my bow and assumed the lead position.

Eerie silence filled the tunnel. *"Drip, drop, drip, drop"*—water leaked from the cracks overhead. My heart rattled my rib cage with each beat, *"thud, thud, thud,"* as I crept into the dark passage.

Deeper into the blackness of the mountain we climbed. I had a strange feeling, like a mouse before a cat ready to pounce.

Large rocks littered the bottom of the cave, making the going slow and the tracking difficult. I held up my hand as I stopped. Eyes wide, I pointed at the Ghost Deer's track pressed deep into the damp clay. Turning, I motioned to Dad, who was coming up from behind.

He smiled and gave me a thumbs up.

Yeah, we're onto you alright, Old Muley... You're not getting away that easy.

Suddenly, an ice-cold droplet landed in my ear, sending chills down my neck. *Could it be venom from a horrific spider or the saliva of a bone-crushing snake?* I didn't dare look up and started shaking my head like a madman, digging in my ear with my finger.

Dad must have thought I'd gone plum mad with all the head shaking. "You alright, bud?" he whispered.

"Oh... yeah, I'm okay, just some water," I said. *Little does he know my tough-guy act is in full throttle.* I faked a hesitant smile.

If he only knew.

Grandpa came up from behind. "Is this incline ever going to end?" he whispered, breathing hard and bending over as he braced his hands against his knees.

Just then, I noticed a dull pain stabbing into my left foot. "I've got a rock in my boot," I whispered. "Can we stop for a minute?"

"Sure," Dad said.

Grandpa nodded, wiping sweat from his forehead and looking grateful.

I leaned my bow against the wall and untied my laces. Raising my foot to waist height, I tried pulling off my boot from a standing position. With one foot up and the other on the ground, I yanked and tugged at my boot with both hands until I lost my balance.

By the way I was hopping and stumbling around, and judging by Dad's ear-to-ear grin, I must have looked like a one-legged drunk flamingo.

As I reached towards the side wall of the cave to catch my balance, my hand landed on a furry, squishy rock, which let out a horrifying screech. My hair about lifted my camo hat right off! I reeled back and jumped so high you would have thought I'd drunk jet fuel for breakfast. During my flight, my whirling arms collided with a whole swarm of the screeching, flapping creatures.

"Bats!" Dad yelled.

The entire ceiling came alive, every crack and crevice feeding the growing mob.

It was as if someone had fired the three of us into a pinball machine, the way we ran around, swinging in every direction, bouncing off walls and each other.

The light from our headlamps spun around the cave as if someone had turned on a strobe light. It was an all-out brawl, and I could not for the life of me tell who was winning.

A bat landed on Dad's face, muffling the string of whoops and yells coming from his mouth. I thought I would do him a favor, so I whirled around and socked it a good one. The bat dropped to the ground, and Dad's eyes crossed so far it looked like they were going to trade places.

Before I could say sorry, another one landed on my head, screeching and pulling at my hair. Now, I had heard of hunts going down badly before, but this was taking it to a new level. As I swatted at my head, a bat latched onto my hand. I started flipping it back and forth so hard I thought my fingers would fly off. His wings flapped with wild fury, as if he were trying to lift me from the ground.

As I flung my hand back, the bat released his grip, shooting off like a bullet, leaving a landing strip through Grandpa's hair.

Wings fluttered and fangs glistened in the beams of light as the black swarm circled.

"Get back-to-back!" Grandpa yelled.

Repositioning, we stopped fighting each other, now ducking and boxing outward in all directions.

This is the end, I thought—*our last battle.*

My arms burned with fury as Dad yelled, "Get down!"

I hit the ground and covered my head. Dad pounded a large rock against the side wall of the cave like a war drum. Loud cracks echoed through the narrow cavern. I glanced up. Dust and rock fragments were exploding with every impact. The bats must have not liked the loud noise, for within seconds, they funneled down the corridor of the cave, their chilling screeches fading into the distance.

Coughing, Grandpa picked up his hat and dusted it off. "Well, that's more excitement than I planned on having!" he said, combing his bat-ruffled hair with his fingers and wiping sweat with his sleeve.

"Tell me about it!" Dad said, rubbing his nose and breathing heavily as he beat dust from his pants.

Gear littered the ground. It looked like someone had dropped a grenade in the middle of us—bows, arrows, packs scattered everywhere. I attempted to catch my breath. My hand throbbed from the many blows it had delivered, and I'd bet the receivers of those blows weren't faring any better.

Amidst my heavy breathing and battle-ridden state, a loud snort echoed through the cave. Startled, I reeled back from my sitting position and collided with the rock-covered ground. Pain shot through my back and I gritted my teeth as the impact flung my headlamp onto the ground. Dad turned, aiming his light in the sound's direction.

I rolled up onto my knees and froze, swallowing hard, barely breathing. Illuminated in the light's beam were the bright blue eyes and white silhouette of the Ghost Deer.

Fog poured from the enormous buck's nostrils as hot breath collided with cool air. He extended his neck, attempting to see through the blinding light. A chill crawled up my back, like an army of spiders.

What should I do?

Turning, I spotted my bow lying against the side of the cave. Dad gave me a nudge, motioning.

Now's the time, I thought.

Slowly, I crawled over and slid an arrow from the quiver. The Ghost Deer snorted, stamping the ground with his hooves. My quavering hand clicked the arrow in softly on the string. I stood, drawing back, attempting to slow my heavy breath. As I adjusted my aim, dread filled my view.

Oh no! I can't see my sight pins! It's too dark!

I raised the bow higher, aligning my arrow with the broad chest of Old Muley. My mind flooded with doubt.

Reed's words haunted me. *"A buck like that would run circles around you. You're just a baby... I doubt you'll even get a buck at all."*

I hadn't practiced without my sight pins for years. Fear seeped in like cold ice. I fought to keep the arrow pointed straight, my arm shaking with adrenaline. Finally, I released, and a sharp *"twang!"* shattered the silence.

The blades glistened as the arrow glided through the darkness—time froze.

Instantly, it struck the ground where the buck once stood. Sparks sprayed as the carbon steel tip dashed across the rock.

"No!" I yelled. "Where did he go? He was right there!" I cried, shaking my finger.

A wave of discouragement and desperation over-whelmed me as I raced into the darkness. After fifty yards, the cave cut to the left.

Dang, where's my headlamp? I cursed inside. My chest heaved, pulling in air. Snatching up a rock, I threw it into the darkness.

"I know you're in there!" I yelled.

Light neared. Dad and Grandpa came alongside, chuckling and ribbing each other.

I snorted in disgust.

This isn't funny! I had the Ghost Deer in sight and I flat out missed him.

Dad gave me a reassuring pat on the back and said, "It's alright, bud. With the little light we have, it was a tough shot."

I shrugged, looking at the ground in defeat. Sighing, I held out my hand. "Did you pick up my headlamp?"

"Maybe…"

"Please."

Dad handed me the headlamp. I secured it on my head and flipped it on. The cave extended another fifty feet, veering to the right. Dust swirled in the light. Stepping forward, I found a track pressed into the clay. "He's still here," I whispered, touching it with my fingers.

A rock rolled in the darkness. I looked up, straining to hear. The sound of antler scraping across rock came from the far end, where the cave twisted out of sight. I glanced at Dad, whose eyes were wide as his hand crawled towards his quiver. Hoofs clattered on rock as an enormous rack of antlers emerged, followed by a white snout and two eyes blazing with glowing fury.

"The Ghost Deer!" I yelled, pointing.

My hand shot to my quiver to retrieve another arrow. Dad and Grandpa came alongside. Together we drew back our bows, forming a blockade. The massive buck snorted, shaking his head, challenging our attack. Stamping his hooves, he dipped his broad antlers and pawed dirt and rock.

"Get ready," Grandpa whispered, straining to hold the bow's tension, "On my mark."

I nodded.

"Ready... aim..."

The buck snorted, bounding forward. A lightning bolt of adrenaline shot through my body at the terrible realization that we were no longer the predator, but now the prey.

With a loud war cry, Grandpa yelled, "Fire!"

The buck leaped into the air, shaking his rack side to side with sharp, jerking motions, preparing to strike.

Three arrows spiraled towards him.

Dad grabbed me, diving to the side. I crashed onto the rock, and a sharp pain shot through my right shoulder. As I rolled onto my back, a flash of white legs and fur soared overhead. Rock fragments sprayed against the side wall of the cave as the monstrous buck landed behind us.

"Clap, clap, clap..." The sound of pounding hooves faded into silence.

Groaning, I turned onto my side to survey the shattered pieces of our victory. With effort I stood and held out my hand to Dad, who was still laying on his back, face tight and eyes closed.

"You, okay?" I asked.

He moaned, looking up at me. "Yeah, just give me a minute." Rolling to his side, he reached behind his back and shoved a rock out of the way, then lay back down.

Propped up against the sidewall of the cave, Grandpa was feeling the back of his head tenderly.

"You alright, Gramps?"

He looked at his hand. "I guess so—a little blood, mostly a goose egg."

Groaning, Dad sat up. "What happened?" he asked.

"Not sure," Grandpa said. "It all played out so fast, I'd barely let go of my string when you slammed me against the wall."

"Let's see if we can find our arrows," Dad said, struggling to stand. I held out my hand. He took it, and I helped him up.

We searched the ground, looking for any sign of a hit. Soon the puzzle pieces came together. A bent arrow here, a broken one there. We found Grandpa's broadhead stuck in a crack in the cave's roof, with what looked like a small tuft of white hair dangling from its feathers. Despite our best efforts, we could not find a speck of blood anywhere.

Defeated, I kicked a rock in disgust. It cracked against the side wall, and I plopped onto the hard earth as the full weight of discouragement set in. I had failed Bandit twice now, and I didn't believe I could do any better.

If I've got to give him to those mean brothers, what will they do to him?

Images of the Bogsleys poking and prodding at Bandit, teasing and tormenting him filled my mind. I envisioned my best friend out in the rain, tied to a stake, standing by a leaky doghouse.

Forgotten, abandoned and alone, Bandit wouldn't understand why I had given up on him. Wouldn't have any reason to. I wanted to cry, but tried to hold it together by tightening my quivering lip, not wanting Dad and Grandpa to think I was a child. I needed to prove I was a man.

"He ran through us like a bunch of sage hens!" I yelled, throwing a rock and waving my hand in the direction the old buck vanished. "I guess he *is* a legend!" I added, partly out of frustration but mostly out of pure realization. We were pursuing this buck with every bit of skill we had, and he was playing us like a cat with a field mouse.

Dad and Grandpa picked up the broken arrows in silence. They looked as discouraged as I felt.

Grandpa's counsel that night on the porch concerning my bet with the Bogsleys came to mind. *Just remember, the only part you have control over is whether you choose to quit or keep trying.'*

I sucked in a heavy breath of muggy air and stood, brushing off my knees. Grandpa looked over, giving me a warm smile.

I wonder if he knows what I'm thinking?

He gave me a nod, as if to say, *"You can do it, Tater; don't give up,"* before waving his hand to encourage me onward.

Deeper into the cave, I searched the ground. The Ghost Deer's tracks were everywhere.

He was here alright. But why did he come back to face us?

Around the corner, the cave twisted to the left, opening into another long tunnel.

Not—trapped? Huh, the Old Muley just wanted a fight, then?

I doubted this was right. Regardless of the reason, the buck wasn't afraid.

A patch of damp ground caught my eye. Something didn't belong. I walked forward and leaned close.

It was a footprint! *But how? Why here?*

I examined it closer.

The Bogsleys? No... How would they ever find this place? How could anyone find it without being led?

The print was large, surely bigger than Reed's or Parley's. Yet, it wasn't a boot. The entire track was smooth, with what appeared to be an imprint of stitches along the outer edges.

A chill raced along my neck, like a breath of cold air. Turning, I ran.

"Dad! Grandpa! Come quick!"

By the time I turned the corner where the buck had come out, they nearly plowed me over.

"What's wrong, Tate?" Dad asked.

"Follow me!" I said, waving. "There's something I want to show you."

An expression of curiosity and relief flashed across Dad's face. "You're okay, then?" he said, grabbing my shoulders and examining me for injury.

"Yeah, I'm fine. I found a track."

"I know, bud. Old Muley's tracks are all over this place."

"No, it's a human track!"

Dad looked at Grandpa, his eyes wide. Turning back to me, he said, "Let's go!"

Soon we were all standing over the footprint.

Grandpa rubbed the back of his neck. "It's human alright. Never seen one like it. If my imagination weren't all stirred up, I'd say it's a moccasin—a big one too!"

"How long do you think it's been here, Gramps?"

"I know it looks fresh, but I'd bet it's sat untouched for a century or two."

"Really? You reckon it's an Indian track?"

"Can't say—but from those petroglyphs we saw back at the entry, I figure it is. It's not every day you get to see an old track like that. Quite a find, Tater, quite a find..."

He gripped my shoulder and looked at his watch. "Well, fellers, we better get going. It's 6:35. To get to the truck before dark, we better head out. We still have quite a hike and a waterfall to get through. I don't know about you, but walking out wet and cold in a forest of pitch-black pines doesn't sound fun to me."

"I agree," Dad said. "The buck's long gone, and if we don't get out in daylight, we'll have a heck of a time finding our way."

"I wish Uncle Sam and his boys were here for all of this," I said, with regret. "We may have gotten the Ghost Deer!"

Grandpa laughed. "You know, Tater, you could be right. They sure have experience with big bucks. However, something tells me this old guy would give even them a Wyoming whirlwind."

"They'll be at base camp tonight, coming in late from Cheyenne," Dad said. "We'll have to see what they say about all this excitement. Something tells me, once those cousins of yours hear the Ghost Deer you've been tooting about is real, they'll wind up like a wild-eyed squirrel."

"Yeah, I bet!" I fired back, laughing. "And all this time, they said *I* was nuts."

Now I have proof, I thought, giving Dad a thumbs up.

Amidst my jubilation, a low rumbling vibrated through the cave. "What's that?" I asked, glancing at Grandpa.

"It's a tremor. Let's hope it doesn't turn into an earthquake," he said.

Thankfully, it soon subsided. "It's time to go!" Grandpa said, his voice anxious. "Let's grab our gear and get out before the mountain eats us for dinner."

CHAPTER 12

A WARM FIRE

The old Ford creaked as the doors shut, sounding as tired as I felt. 10:35 pm, far too late to be dragging in. By the time we'd made it out of the cave, half drowned again in the waterfall and become lost, it was everything we could do to find the truck and return to camp.

"Welcome back!" Uncle Sam said in his deep, billowy voice. Waving my hand, I staggered towards the roaring fire, approaching the warm light. He stroked his dark beard and laughed. "Thought we might have to go save your hides."

"Sorry, guys," Grandpa said. "We weren't sure if we would make it back either." He plopped into the nearest chair by the fire, huffing out a deep, well-deserved sigh.

Dad walked over to the cooler. "Do you want one?" he said, pointing at a dripping can.

I perked up. "You bet."

Grandpa nodded.

Dad threw us each a soda. "Thanks for starting the fire," he said, popping his open. He took a sip and held out his hand to the glowing flames.

"Sure is a welcome sight," Grandpa agreed, kicking his feet up on a rock and leaning back.

Uncle Sam smiled. "No problem, we just got in an hour ago."

Carter, the younger of my two older cousins, adjusted his camo hat over his curly blond hair. "Did you see anything?"

113

My sleep-heavy eyes lit up. "Did we see anything?" I said. "Oh, just the biggest buck you've ever laid eyes on!"

Brock grinned, his square jawline and short-cropped hair illuminated in the firelight. He leaned forward. "Oh really? What did he look like?" he asked, giving Carter a poke in the ribs with his elbow.

"No, I'm serious! We saw the Ghost Deer!"

"The white buck you've been bragging about?"

"That's the one, except this time I saw more than a glimpse. I stared him down, at thirty yards."

"If you saw him that close, where is he now?" Carter asked, poking a stick at the fire.

"How should I know? That monster buck could be anywhere."

He chuckled. "Yeah, I noticed he wasn't in the back of the Ford."

I sighed, lowering my head and kicking at the dirt.

By the time Brock and Carter got done probing me about the old buck, and thanks to Grandpa and Dad confirming the truth, my older cousins were as lit up as the fire itself.

Uncle Sam ran his fingers through his beard, eyes squinted and forehead crinkled. "Really?" he questioned. "You're not pulling our legs now, are you?"

"Serious," Dad said, "white as a ghost! It was like he had gnarled branches of antlers coming out of his head."

Sam stood, stretching his back. "Man! You've even got me excited. It's been a while since any buck has raised my eyebrows."

I then told them about the thieving squirrel, the wild-eyed mama moose, and our run-in with the bats. They laughed and asked a lot of questions.

"Well, it sounds like you've had one heck of a day!" Uncle Sam said.

Grandpa coughed. "You better believe it! It about put me in hunting retirement—almost the grave." He stood, hunching over, apparently stiff and exhausted. He tossed his pop can into the trash and stretched. "I'm going to water the bushes and head to bed. You guys wore me right out," he said as he made his way into the pines, disappearing into the darkness.

Brock stood and grabbed a couple of logs from the woodpile, throwing them on the fire. Within moments, the flames rose high, crackling and popping, extending their warmth.

I had a big problem. My front was too hot and my rear end felt like it had an ice block strapped to it. I stood, facing my back to the fire.

"You guys have me all riled up on this big buck and his antlers," Brock said. "I won't sleep a lick tonight."

"Me either!" Carter agreed, flicking a stick towards the fire with his fingers. "This muley you're describing sounds like nothing I've ever heard of."

Just then, Grandpa came charging through camp, holding up his pants and running like he had seen a ghost. "Skunk!" he yelled, pointing behind.

In an instant, everything shot into commotion. I about fell into the fire, stumbling and flapping my arms for balance. Dad bolted from his chair so suddenly it flipped back, tripping Brock as he ran past, ejecting him into the air. Carter, hot on his heels, received a boot to the chin, and Brock toppled into the brush.

From there, it just got worse. The skunk waddled into camp, tail straight up, hissing and pawing at the ground.

This was all Dad needed to wave the white flag of retreat, busting out in a run.

The problem was—I didn't. I just stood there like a frozen statue as his shoulder caught my side, spinning me around. My head felt like it was floating away as I whirled around with my arms out, attempting to keep my balance. Images of black and white skunk mixed with flashes of fire filled my view.

I was disoriented and staggering, and none of the options of escape seemed worth having.

"Tater, get out of there!" Sam yelled.

About then, my spinning world slowed enough to see the skunk right in front of me. He whipped around and shot up his tail.

Suddenly, I almost swallowed my eyeballs as powerful arms crushed the air from my lungs like a bear hugging a side of beef, launching me through the air. The ground approached fast as I crashed into the brush. Cracking and popping sounds filled my ears, and sharp pain clawed at my face and head.

In an instant, it stopped, and I found myself face down, coughing out dirt. The solid grip released and smothering weight rolled off, allowing me to gulp mouthfuls of air. Breathing hard and coughing, Uncle Sam lay beside me in the grass.

He turned his head in my direction. In a scratchy voice, he asked, "You okay, Tater?"

I moaned, rolling onto my back. "Not sure," I said, gritting my teeth. "It feels like I just got run over by a truck."

He grinned, wiping blood from the corner of his mouth and spitting out dirt. "That's because you did. If the skunk had sprayed you, your hunting days this season would've been over."

I sat up, holding my stomach. "Well, thank you, then—I guess," I said, my jaw still tight. "I reckon getting steamrolled is better than missing out on the hunt."

He chuckled. "Spoken like a true hunter." He groaned and got to his feet. Sam held out his hand. "Here, let me help you up."

CHAPTER 13
A NEW DAY

The next morning, the alarm went off at 4:00 am, pounding in my head like a fire alarm. My eyes were heavy and my body ached. "Just a few more minutes," I protested.

Dad turned over, swatted the alarm, and fell back into bed. He sighed. "I wish, bud, I could use some more sleep." He lay in silence as my heavy eyes started dragging me back to sleep. Dad sat up, groaned, and stretched. "Tater, if you want to be in position during prime time, we've got to get up."

As I lay burrowed in my warm sleeping bag, excitement for another chance to see the white buck seeped into my mind, bringing life to my clouded thoughts.

"Dang skunk!" I whispered.

"What did you say?" Dad asked.

"Oh, nothing. Just upset about the skunk last night. He about got me killed, you know."

Dad chuckled. "Killed?"

"Yeah, I think Uncle Sam almost broke my ribs, saving me from a mouthful of skunk spray."

Dad's forehead crinkled as he raised an eyebrow. "Was it wrong that he helped?" he asked.

I huffed, trying to release the churning emotion. "I guess I should be grateful. I just wish it hadn't happened."

Dad looked at me for a moment, his eyes soft, but his face firm. "You know, Tater, a lot of stuff in life doesn't happen the way we want. In fact, some of it goes exactly how we don't want, but you can't let it cloud your vision of the truth."

"What truth?"

"Things end up being how they need to be to help us grow."

"Grow!?" I exclaimed. "Can't I just grow the way I want? I don't need to get steamrolled to grow!"

"The thing is, Tater, how we need to grow isn't always how we want to grow."

I considered that for a moment.

"What did you learn from last night?" Dad asked.

"I hate skunks! And—Uncle Sam should have played football! That's what I got out of it!"

Dad chuckled, "Okay, you've got me there, but what else?"

"What is there to learn? It just happened, and I hope it doesn't happen again," I said, heaving my feet over the side of the bed onto the cold trailer floor.

"Well, we can always hope, Tater," Dad said. "However, there is something to be grateful for."

"I guess so." I agreed. "I'm just glad I didn't get sprayed."

He smiled as he scratched the back of his neck. "So am I!" He set his hand on my shoulder and asked, "What about the fact the skunk hightailed it from camp after Sam tackled you?"

"Yes, I was glad to see him gone," I replied.

"You know, Tater, Uncle Sam stepped in the line of fire for you and got battered up himself."

"I guess you're right."

He stretched and stood up. "Now let's get moving. We have a full day ahead, and with how stirred up you got Brock and Carter last night, I bet they're standing at our door right now, bows in hand."

Grandpa sat up from the side bunk, rubbing his hand across his eyes and mustache. "Can't you guys keep it down and let a feller get some shuteye?" he said, chuckling. "I'm getting too old for this adventure business."

"Oh, come on, Grandpa… it's not all that bad. It keeps you out of doing chores back home."

He chuckled. "You've got a point. If I weren't here getting dragged around the hills with you all, that blasted rooster would toot his horn back home anyway." He yawned, ran his fingers through his iron gray hair and stood, displaying the full glory of his red thermal underwear as he scratched his chest. "Well, let's go see what we can find."

CHAPTER 14

THE TRAPPER

I soon found myself back in the high mountain basin where we had first seen the Ghost Deer. The sun was cresting the towering cliffs, and the morning dew had already soaked through my pant legs.

"So, where was he at?" Sam asked.

"Just down by the river," I said, pointing. "See the pool by the waterfall?"

"Yep."

"He went right in."

"I'm still having a hard time believing it."

"Should we try the cave again?" I asked.

"I doubt it," Sam replied, scanning the area. "Since you chased him in there, he's likely going to be hiding somewhere you've never been. A buck of this caliber doesn't take chances." Pointing, he said, "Let's head to the river and see what the tracks have to say."

With some effort, we made it to the river's edge. Working our way through the willows, we soon found a large lodgepole pine that had blown across the river. Several branches blocked our way. Uncle Sam pulled a hatchet from his pack, and within minutes, we had a clear path. Though my boots were still wet and squishy from the day before, I was grateful we didn't have to wade the river.

After about a half hour, we were on the far bank by the waterfall.

"Man, look at those tracks!" Carter said, pointing.

"Wow!" Sam said. "You sure this was a deer?"

"You better believe it," Grandpa confirmed. "Big as an elk! He's a deer alright... maybe some kind of hybrid."

Sam shook his head, bending over to examine the prints closer. "This guy must be ancient!"

He scanned the ground, walking away from the river. "Looks like when he left the cave, he headed into those thick pines over there," he said, pointing.

After some discussion, we followed the tracks. I suspected the old buck was long gone by now, but I just couldn't let go of the dream of seeing him again. From what I could tell, the others felt the same. Buck fever had its hold.

Shortly after entering the pines, we lost the tracks, but we kept heading in the general direction. The way the squirrels and chipmunks were chattering, you would have thought we had stolen their favorite pine nut.

I sighed and scanned the nearby treetops. *Darn critters. So much for staying silent.*

Upon breaking through the darkness of the pines, we entered a large meadow. At the far end, smoke climbed through the trees, twisting into the sky.

"Fire!" I said, pointing.

Dad shielded his eyes from the sun. "I wonder what it could be?"

"May have been lightning last night," Grandpa said. "I've never seen anyone else this high." He chuckled. "Come to think of it, I've never been in this far myself."

As we came closer to the rising smoke, I stopped. "Hey, look over there. It's a little cabin. See it? There in the trees?"

"Yeah, looks handmade," Grandpa said. "My eyes aren't doing too well, but it looks like there are ax marks all over the logs."

"You're right," Dad agreed. "See the notched-out corners and clay chinking filling the cracks?"

As we crept closer, the cabin's rooftop came into view, covered in small logs lashed together and blanketed with green sod. On the side, a tall rock chimney rose above its peak.

"Hey, look there!" I said, pointing. "See the poles with furs and hides strung between the trees?"

"Yeah, I see them," Grandpa said.

"Hold it right there!" an old crackling voice called out from behind us.

I spun around to find the end of a rifle pointed in our direction. "Drop them bows!" the man said, motioning with his gun. "Come on now, hurry it up—I don't have patience for

thieves!" We did as he asked. "Now put them arms up, yeah…
that's right, where I can see 'em. Don't want you reachin for
your knives."

The old man scratched his chin through his long,
mangy white beard. Above his squinted eyes sat a pair of
shaggy eyebrows, as if two caterpillars had climbed up on his
face. Deep-cut wrinkles branched out from the corners of his
upper cheekbones. And the coonskin hat he wore was thick
and bushy, with the critter's face in front, as if he had a second
pair of eyes.

"Thought you could pull one over on old Jasper, did
ya?" he said, shoving the rifle at Dad's chest.

"What are you talking about, sir?" Dad said. "We don't
mean any harm."

"Sir? Hah! I haven't never been called no sir. Tryin to
grab my hides, are you? It's taken me pert near a year to put
this stash together."

Grandpa stepped forward, hands above his head.
"Jasper, we're just out hunting. We saw the smoke and had a
look. If you'll be so kind as to drop that gun, we'll leave you
be."

127

"Huntin, you say? What you hunting fer?"

"Deer," Sam said. "A great white buck."

The old man eyed us, as if trying to probe our souls. He laughed, dry and hoarse, his face softening as he lowered his gun. "Oh… you're chasin the Guardian, are ya?"

"The Guardian?" Dad questioned… "You mean the Ghost Deer?"

"Ah, call him what you want, but I know what he is. Come on in the cabin and sit for a spell. I can save you all some time. It's a might bit lonely here in these hills. I could use the company." Dad and Sam looked at Grandpa. He nodded. We grabbed our bows and followed the old hermit to his cabin.

As the door creaked open, musty smells of meat and fur penetrated my nostrils. The one-room cabin was dark, with only candlelight in the far corner. A simple bed with a lashed-together frame covered in deer and beaver pelts sat against the far end of the room, while steel traps of various sizes hung from rusted nails along the walls.

Jasper cleared off a pair of snowshoes from a long bench made of logs and set them to the side. "Just making some repairs," he said. "Got to be gettin ready for winter.

Comes a might bit early in these parts." Dusting the bench off with his coonskin hat, he pointed to a couple of chairs surrounding a log table in the corner. "Sit a spell. I'll pour you some juniper berry tea." Picking up a rusted tin can, he rattled it. "You want some pine nuts while you wait?"

I looked at Dad. He nodded, so I held out my hand.

Jasper smiled, revealing his tarnished teeth with black gaps. From the looks of it, I assumed some of those teeth must have jumped right out, figuring there was a better place to go. He sprinkled the pine nuts in my hand. I popped them in my mouth.

They weren't as tasty as I remembered. I had eaten some at Grandpa's a few years back, yet Jasper hadn't roasted these. They were dry on the outside and chewy on the inside, tasting stale and dusty.

"I'll be right back," he said. "Need to snatch that tea from the fire."

Soon as Jasper left, I scrunched up my nose and put my hands around my throat, making a gagging sign to Brock, who was about ready to help himself to the can.

Dad motioned for me to quit. "Be polite," he whispered. "Remember, he's a little trigger-happy."

Just then, the door flew open. I scooted back on the bench and straightened.

"Here, youngling, have yourself some tea," Jasper said, handing me a tin cup. He poured the steaming green liquid into the cup as I adjusted my hand onto the handle, attempting to relieve my grip from the heat.

I smiled weakly and nodded.

He grinned, nodding with excitement. "Well, now— have a sip. It'll put hair on your chest."

I looked over at Grandpa, and he gave me an encouraging nod.

The hot liquid seared my tongue with biting heat and bitter flavor, causing me to pucker. It tasted like a boiled pine bough with a bit of lemon.

He laughed, dry and gravelly. "Got a punch to it, don't it?"

I coughed, pressing my lips together, nodding in agreement. I wanted to dump it out under the bench when he wasn't looking, but, afraid he might catch me, I forced myself to sip it politely.

After Jasper poured a cupful for the rest of the crew, he sat on the bed and faced us, sipping on his own cup.

"You live here all the time?" Sam asked.

"Course I do," Jasper said. "Goin on pert near forty years."

Grandpa blew on his hot tea. "A long time to be alone in these woods."

"Sure is, but it's my home. Hard to remember anything else."

"From all the furs, looks like you're a trapper," Dad said, motioning to the pelts scattered around the cabin.

"A trapper I am. I've gotta keep going farther to find those varmints, though. The wolves aren't helping none either."

"There are wolves up here?" I asked, looking at Dad with concern.

"Yeah, we've got a pack of them suckers! Been causing me a lot of grief."

"What do you mean?" Grandpa questioned.

"They like to eat my pelts, with the critters right in 'em. They're not leaving me much to eat either. I've gotten a few of 'em with old Lou here," he said, holding up his lever-action rifle. "But it's cost me."

"How's that?" Grandpa asked.

Jasper sat the rifle beside him. He then rolled up the sleeve of his deerhide jacket. I recoiled at the sight. A large, pink scar extended along his forearm, sunken in at the center.

"What happened?" Brock asked, pointing.

"This here's what happens when Scar Face takes a bite out of your arm." Then, lifting his beard, he turned his neck. A long, jagged scar extended from his ear to the base of his jawline.

"Thought I was a goner," he said. "Would've been too, if that alpha wolf had his way of it."

"How'd you make it out alive?" Sam asked, swatting a fly from the back of his neck.

"Well—let me tell ya. Old Jasper here was up, checking his lines on the upper fork, where the rivers join. It's about a mile as the crow flies up yonder," he said, pointing to the north. "The snow was about knee-high and I'd gotten me a beaver—a big one too. I was on my knees next to the river, trying to get the potbellied varmint out of my froze-up trap, when I heard something moving behind me. I turned just in time for old Scar Face to sink his teeth into this here arm."

"Why didn't you shoot him?" I questioned.

Jasper laughed, taking his coonskin hat off and hanging it on the corner of the bed. He ran his fingers through his sweat-laden gray hair, then looked at me for a long, hard minute.

"Look here, young feller, I'm no fool," he said. "I had old Lou here with me," he added, pointing to the rifle. "The problem was, I had her propped against a tree about three feet away. I reached for my gun but couldn't grab her, so I thumped him on the head with my free arm."

"Did he let go?" I asked.

Jasper laughed. "Hah, if only it was that easy. Old Scar Face is a big old boy, a powerful monster of a wolf. He wasn't about to let me have my fire stick. So, he shook his head around and tore through my jacket," he said, pulling his sleeve down and pointing to a large patch on the arm. "Took a piece of my arm with it. Then he went for my neck—had me in a death hold, he did. I struggled for as long as I could, before everything went black."

"What happened?" Carter asked. "Where did the wolves go? How'd you get free?"

"Can't say for sure. I woke up to the sound of wind howling through pines and the bubbling of a lonely river. I rolled onto my stomach and struggled to get up. By then, the sun was behind those mountains," Jasper said, waving his hand westward. "Wolf sign was everywhere. From the pushed-up snow, it looked like something landed thirty feet away, sliding on its side. I figured it might have been the old gray wolf. Snow was knee deep, and I had a hard time finding readable tracks, but I could tell one set didn't belong."

"What'd they look like?" I asked.

"By the way they bounced in and bounced out, they were deer. But I suspect not just any deer."

"What do you mean?" Grandpa questioned. "If it wasn't a deer, what was it?"

"Well... based on the size of them tracks, and the way they were twenty feet apart, I reckon it was the white buck. By the time I got back to camp, I was about all bled out, sicker than a porcupine on wormwood. I barely made it through the winter. If it weren't for a stash of smoked meat, homemade whiskey, and a lot of praying, you'd have found a skeleton lying in this here bed."

"You really believe the Ghost Deer saved you?" I asked.

"Sure do! Me and him have an understanding now. I tried just like you to take that old buck. He taunted me for years, outsmarting me every time. Shoot, now I recall, he's been around for as long as I can remember."

"He's that old?" Brock questioned.

"Sure is. I first saw him when I was a young man. He was white back then and still as big as ever. I can't explain it. Never tried to, always just accepted it for what it was."

There was silence for a time. I figured everyone was doing the same thing I was, trying to swallow everything old Jasper had said.

"So, I'm guessing you call him the Guardian, on account of him saving your life?" I asked.

"Well... yeah, to me, he is a guardian."

"I can see that," I replied.

"So, what do you say about us hunting him, then?" Carter asked.

Jasper slapped his knee, rocked back, and belted out a deep belly laugh. "Have at it, boys! I won't stop ya. Just know old Jasper here's given you a fair warning. You're not dealing with no ordinary buck."

I guess I had already come to realize this, but to hear the old trapper's stories just made it more real.

Grandpa stood and stretched his back. "Well, Jasper, it's been mighty polite of you to give us some rest and hospitality. We wish you much luck in your trapping this winter, but we best be moving on."

As we left the cabin, Carter, a trapper himself, walked over to look at the furs on the lines, admiring their beauty and stroking their softness. "What are you going to do with all these pelts?" he asked.

"I'll be trading for them, of course. Been working on tanning all summer."

"Who do you trade with up here?" Carter asked. "Seems like you don't get to town much."

Jasper hesitated. "My old truck's still down yonder," he said, pointing. "Rusted out and filled with grass. I haven't left for years. Yeah, at first I would go to town for supplies now and then—until I figured out how to live off the land and make a living with these here furs. I stockpiled enough ammo to last a lifetime."

"Who do you trade with then?" Carter persisted.

Jasper went silent, his face uneasy as he ran his hand through his beard, looking at the ground. Then, taking a deep breath, he looked up, glaring at Carter like a cornered cougar, eyes hard and jaw tight.

"Boy..." he said, sucking in a deep breath of air and gritting his teeth. "I'll not be telling you who I'm trading with, but you all might want to steer clear of the mountain there," he said, nodding to the cliffs. "It'd be for your own good to find somewhere else to hunt."

"Why?" I asked. "We've already been over there. Even followed the buck through the waterfall."

Jasper's face contorted. "You what!?"

"Yeah... we've been inside the mountain. No big deal... Buck about ran us over, but we're alright."

"You went in and came back out?"

"Yeah, there's a cave under the waterfall—over there by the river."

"Huh? What did you find?"

"Some petroglyphs, bats and the Old Muley—who about killed us."

"Interesting—Nothing else?"

"There was an old Indian track that was kind of neat, but nothing else. Why?"

Jasper sighed, stroking his beard and looking at the ground. "Well… consider yourselves lucky then." Pointing at the cliffs, he added, "Regardless, I'd keep away none the same if I were you. You watch yourselves now… you best be getting off."

"Are we in danger?" Grandpa asked.

"I've already said too much," Jasper said, running his fingers through his matted hair. Then he waved his hand. "Go on now—and keep your eyes open. Let's just say I wasn't the first one here."

CHAPTER 15
PAINFUL MEMORIES

As we left the cabin, heading north into the thick pines, my chest felt like a rock was sitting on it. Jasper's words had sucked the hope right out of me, dashing my dreams of ever getting the buck.

"Where are we going now?" I asked. "Jasper sounded like we'd be in for it if we went back to the cliffs," I said, waving my hand in their direction. "Crazy old man! He's been here so long he's plum lost his mind."

Dad stopped and turned to look at me. "Tate, we don't know what state of mind old Jasper's in, or what he may hide, but there's no need for name-calling."

"He's hiding something alright."

"He's just trying to protect us," Dad said.

"From what?"

"Apparently, he's trading those furs with someone, and he's set on keeping it to himself."

I huffed, biting my tongue. The sun, now lower in the sky, brought a sense of urgency, which gnawed at my bones.

Gosh, how much time have we wasted? I wish we had never gone by the old cabin. Jasper almost shot us anyway. He sure was protective of those furs—the old codger.

I kicked at a mounded ant pile, spraying sand across a nearby bush. "That's it!" I said, "It's over! I don't even know why we're out here anymore!"

"What are you talking about?" Dad said. "Why are you giving up now?"

"Why do you think? Jasper crushed my hopes of ever getting the Ghost Deer. He's been hunting him for years—with his rifle, too! What chance do I, or any of us, have against a buck like that? These bows are nothing! For heaven's sake, Dad! He said the buck saved his life. I don't even know what to believe."

A breeze rustled the trees as I adjusted my camo jacket tighter around my neck.

"Tater, what makes you think success is only bringing home Old Muley?" Uncle Sam asked with firmness. "There are plenty of animals up here. Maybe we'll see the Ghost Deer again, maybe we won't, but you can't just quit because you're believing the lies rattling around in your head. Any buck I've ever harvested has taken plenty of skin off my feet and put sweat on my back. There's been many a year I've come home with nothing but blisters and grand memories."

Uncle Sam's words stung, but I took them to heart. Here was a man I believed to be like Daniel Boone, tall, strong, with loads of big bucks hanging on his wall. *How could he say such a thing? No Ghost Deer?! Why be out here, then?*

Then it hit me. *Why am I out here? ... Bandit! How could I have gotten so wrapped up in the old muley? Have I completely forgotten my best friend?* Buck fever and bragging rights had consumed me, while all the time Bandit's fate lay squarely on my shoulders.

I wondered if the Bogsleys were tracking us. Likely dressed in camo themselves, they would be hard to spot. With the size and strength of our crew, they would stay out of sight—at least until they found the Ghost Deer themselves or caught me alone.

Painful memories flooded my mind like drops of lava beating on my chest. It felt as if I were there all over again as my mind took me back.

*   *   *

BOGSLEY PROPERTY, MAY 13*th*, 1984

Parley pulled on Bandit's ears as he yelped out in pain, attempting to free himself from the tangled fence lining the Bogsleys' property.

"Leave him alone!" I yelled, dropping my bike into the tall grass along the road.

"Awe, ain't he so cute," Parley said, pulling on Bandit's face.

He thrashed around, bellowing out a howl as the barbed wire sank deeper into his hide.

"I said, get away!"

Grabbing Parley by the back of his dirt-covered T-shirt, I yanked hard. Falling off balance, he landed on top of me. Pain

142

shot through my nose as his body smashed my head into the dirt.

Rolling off, he stood, swatting at his pants.

"Hah, thought you could teach me some manners, did ya?" he said, kicking dirt at me.

I curled up, holding my head as the taste of blood filled my mouth. Pain throbbed through my skull and my ears buzzed. I tried to stand, but Parley shoved me back down.

"Have some of your own medicine?" he said through gritted teeth. "I was only playing with that dog there."

"You weren't playing. You were hurting him. And you know it!" I said, spitting out blood and dirt.

He laughed in a cold-hearted way that made my blood boil. "Hah, so what if I was? It's my fence and my property, and I'll do with it what I please."

I stood, staggering, attempting to gain balance. "Let him go, Parley!" I said, pointing at Bandit. "You've had your fun."

"Oh, yeah... maybe I will. But it's going to cost ya!"

"What?"

"How about that bike there?" he said, pointing at my shiny red BMX, a birthday gift from Mom and Dad only a month before.

"You want me to give you my new bike so I can free my dog?"

"Yeah, how about it?"

I stepped forward, clenching my fist.

"I wouldn't do that if I were you," Reed said, coming up from behind.

"Fine! You can borrow my bike."

"I said have!" Parley growled, spitting on the ground.

Bandit whimpered, struggling against the barbed wire, as his sorrowful black eyes stared up at me.

"Well, do I have me a bike?" Parley asked, brushing back his tangled blond hair.

"Borrow," I whispered, dropping my head in defeat.

*   *   *

About three months later, I caught them with their guard down, snatched up my bike and fled for home. No longer shiny, my once-prized possession now scratched with a bent frame.

No, Bandit—I won't quit. Not now, not ever.

This I promised to myself as I followed the men deeper into the depths of the forest.

CHAPTER 16
FACE TO FACE

We climbed the hillside, following a worn deer trail. To my dismay, we found no sign or tracks resembling the Ghost Deer. We soon came to a meadow filled with aspens, fallen trees, and a few boulders. A small stream glistened in the sunlight at the far end.

The area looked promising, stretching back a couple hundred yards, narrowing as it blended into the tall pines.

146

"We should start splitting up," Sam said. "There are fresh signs throughout this area. Looks like a good bet for the night."

Dad scratched the stubble on his face, examining the meadow. "Good idea. Tater, why don't you and I take this one?"

Despite the promising features, the first spot never felt like the best spot.

"Why can't I go higher? We just got here, and our scent has already blown back in there," I said, waving my hand in the meadow's direction.

He motioned to the late-afternoon sun. "We're running out of time, bud. We need to be in position before the deer move."

I folded my arms, stiffening. "Can I at least hunt this myself, then?"

"You ready?" Dad asked.

My face felt hot. Carter smirked, nudging Brock. I hated being the youngest. Always felt like I had something to prove. "Of course I am!" I said, not believing it myself. "Why do you think I've been practicing all this time? I'll be just fine."

147

Dad hesitated, rubbing the back of his neck. "Alright, but be careful.

Smiling, he swatted me on the back. "We'll head up this trail and spread out along the way. I'll take the next spot. Stay here until we come back. If you need help, holler. I should be close enough to hear."

I nodded, faking a smile.

As I watched them hike over the hill, my stomach churned as the reality of being alone set in. Determined to show the guys I could run with the pack, I soon found a large boulder surrounded by thick brush in the meadow's corner. I climbed on the rock and nocked an arrow.

Water trickled through the nearby stream, masking much of the forest sounds. A squirrel chattered in the distance, and a cool breeze rustled the leaves overhead. The shadows of tall pines stretched across the meadow.

I quietly zipped my jacket, looped my arm through my bow, and placed my hands in my pockets.

Alone, deep in the forest, a man has a lot of time to dream. My mind swirled with images of wolves running, jumping over fallen trees, and weaving around brush as they chased the white buck. The ghost-like mule deer bounded across the small stream, spraying droplets of water high into the air, the wolves hot on his heels.

"Dang those wolves," I whispered. *They better not get to the Old Muley before I do.*

I wondered if the wolves were still in the area. I hadn't seen tracks, but I knew they migrated great distances. With luck, they were now far away.

With my older cousins Brock and Carter joining us, I had something to prove. I'd always looked up to them—liked them, too. Carter taught me to fly fish one year, and Brock was always kind. Yet, since I didn't have brothers, I felt pressure and anxiety creeping in. *What if they get a buck, and I don't? What if their bucks are bigger than mine?*

I realized these thoughts were selfish, yet they were still very real to me.

A branch broke and a squirrel chattered downhill to my right. Closing my eyes, I strained to enhance my ability to hear. Another crash came from below.

Gripping my bow tight, I adjusted my position, nestling into the brush.

Something huge is coming.

Sweat beaded on my forehead.

More squirrels chattered, protesting at the intruder's presence. My breath became heavy, increasing in speed as a cold droplet trickled down the back of my collar.

My body jolted as a loud crack cut through the air near the tree line. About sixty yards away, movement caught my eye. I focused on a section of trees at the meadow's edge.

I couldn't decide whether I should stand or remain sitting. The distance was out of my range. If I stood, I would risk being seen, and a shot at this yardage would surely end in defeat.

I glimpsed what I thought was antler tines moving through the thick trees, though I wasn't sure. My adrenaline surged. More movement, another loud crack. I went to pull back my bow, but reconsidered. Now would be the best time to prevent detection. But I knew I couldn't hold the draw long.

My straining eyes burned with desire.

What if it stays in the trees? What if it smells me before I get a shot?

My mind raced as impatience tugged at my will. Part of me wanted to move closer, the other part wanted to run.

Suddenly, a large bull moose emerged. My hopes dropped like an egg splattering on the rock.

"No!" I cursed under my breath.

The bull's dark mane and thick neck rippled as he flinched, attempting to shake off a fly. He lowered his head and wide spoon-shaped antlers. Stepping forward, he ripped out a mouthful of vegetation.

I froze, surprised he was unaware of my presence.

Darn moose! Any other time, this would have been a treat.

An impressive sight, yet, so set on finding a buck, I only saw him as an obstacle. While he was here munching in my meadow, I was certain the deer would stay away. Even if they came, the moose would spot me—ruining everything.

I scowled at the unwanted guest, attempting to remain a motionless, frustrated statue. Gradually, the moose worked his way up the hill, pulling out thick mouthfuls of grass. When he was thirty yards away, my feelings transitioned from frustration to unease.

Crud! What should I do? I questioned. *If I stand up, I'll spook him and he may charge. If I keep sitting, he'll probably come closer.*

I was like a mouse, trapped in the corner of a room the cat hadn't yet discovered. Though I could run, the moose could run faster.

Will I have to shoot in self-defense? I wondered.

Suddenly, the moose's head shot up as he craned his neck high. Snorting, he sucked in deep breaths of air, shaking his massive antlers.

Probing different directions, he swung around, his black eyes piercing me like a lance. My spine tingled, and I found it difficult to breathe.

Sounds of crunching grass and breaking twigs grew louder as the monstrous bull walked towards me. Petrified, my body became one with the rock. I stared forward, without a blink.

As the moose neared, he cocked his head, drawing in deep breaths of air. The ground vibrated under his weight. The bull's coal-like eyes and long snout were right in front of me now. My bow sat on my lap with the arrow pointing in his direction, the tip of my broadhead inches away from his chest.

I wondered what he would do if it poked him. My eyes burned, still unblinking as tears streamed from the corners. I sat rigid as a stump, not daring to breathe.

A fly landed on my nose, tickling. I felt like I would explode if I didn't swat it off. Yet, there was the moose, staring and sniffing, so close the heat of his body warmed the air in front of me.

My goal was to convince my pursuer I was part of the rock, though I smelled like a human.

Impossible... I thought. *He has a nose like a bloodhound.*

The moose stared as he cocked his head, examining me with his piercing black eyes. Snorting softly, he leaned closer, dipping within a foot of my face. Nostrils flaring, he probed deeper. A stench of hot decomposing grass filled my nostrils. I wanted to vomit, but fought the urge. My lungs burned for air. One swipe of his mighty rack would crush me, and with a stomp of his hoof, my leg would break.

Images flashed through my mind: kneeling with my family, praying in the comfort of our home. I wondered if it was a message. I needed a miracle. Yet, the only person I could call to for help was God. So… I prayed.

God—please help me! I pleaded in silence. *I hope you're there… and I sure hope you hear me. This bull is going to kill me, and I'm trapped. Please… please help!*

A rivulet of sweat trickled down my forehead, stinging my eye. Everything in my body told me to blink, and everything in my mind fought it.

The moose lifted his head and massive spoon-shaped antlers high, sampling the air in all directions with his long snout. A shadow fell upon me as the monstrous bull glared— his dark eyes penetrating. He craned his neck forward, his nose now inches from my face. Tears seeped out, rolling down my cheek.

Suddenly, the bull jerked back, turning to the east and then to the west, sniffing and snorting—appearing bewildered. From his actions, it was as if I could read his thoughts… *"This rock smells like a human, but it's not alive! Is this a trap? Are they after me…?"*

154

He snorted loudly, spraying droplets of warm mucus on my face. Pawing at the ground, he swung around, grunted, and scanned the forest. He then shook his neck and bellowed, lunging forward as he crashed into the brush and thundered off into the forest. Within moments, he disappeared into the thick vegetation, followed by the sounds of rustling trees and snapping branches.

Exhaling a burst of painful air, I sucked in deep gulps of refreshing breath and wiped my face with shaking hands.

I can't believe it! I fooled him! I thought as I slid off the rock.

I paused. Though the moose was no longer around, something didn't feel right. *Was it a miracle from God...?* I replayed the events in my mind. *Did I really trick that old bull?* I sighed. *How could I?* Though none of it made sense, I knew what had happened.

CHAPTER 17
NOT ALONE

My stomach felt raw and my head spun as the oversupply of adrenaline coursed through my veins. Relieved at being freed from the bull moose, I staggered to the river, kneeled, and splashed cold water onto my face, wiping it dry with my sleeve.

As I was about to stand, something caught my eye. I leaned over, examining the ground. In the mud a few feet away was a large track, about the size of my hand, with a big depression in the back, and claw marks extending from four smaller pads in the front.

"Wolves?"

I shot to my feet, scanning the area. *The track looks fresh, likely this morning.* I examined the stream's edge and found several other tracks of various sizes, none as large as the first.

"They're here!" I whispered.

The sun sat low in the west, and Dad and the guys weren't back yet. He'd told me to stay put until they came for me. Yet, after almost getting clobbered by a moose, and now seeing the wolf tracks… I didn't want to be alone.

I followed the stream up another fifteen feet and froze as a flash of shock tore through my nerves. There, in the mud beside the river, was a large human track, smooth, with faint imprints of stitching along the outer edges. "Just like the one in the cave," I whispered.

My eyes frantically scanned the surrounding trees. *Could it be Jasper? He runs traplines, but why would he have been in the cave, too?* I wondered.

The meadow felt eerie. Like something or someone was watching me. Not far off, a branch snapped as a flash of red disappeared behind a tree. *The Bogsleys?* I questioned.

I rushed back, grabbed my gear, and leaped over the stream. I soon found the trail and sprinted in the direction I'd last seen the guys.

Within minutes, I crested the hilltop, sucking in deep gulps of air. The path dropped into the trees. Branches clawed at me as I ran, like hands reaching for a prisoner. Accelerating in speed, I raced deeper into the woods. I couldn't tell if someone was chasing me, but it felt that way.

As I rounded the corner, a grouse shot up from a nearby bush, startling me. I tripped, tumbling forward as I released my bow, belly flopping onto the dirt. Gasping for air, I attempted to get up. Sounds of pounding footsteps increased. A twig broke, the thudding of feet became louder, fast approaching. As I pushed myself to my knees, my hands stung. I tried to see who was coming, but burning dust filled my eyes. A shadow approached, then two powerful hands grabbed my arms, pulling me to my feet.

"Looks like you've seen a ghost, Tater," Dad said, dusting me off. "You okay, bud?"

I exhaled a sigh of relief, hugging him tight. My voice cracked as I attempted to speak. In a whisper, I said, "I'm okay now."

CHAPTER 18
THE BUCK

"I about got killed, Dad."

His face became serious as he looked me over.

"You what?"

"Yeah, I was face to face with a moose!"

His brows raised. "Glad you're alright," he said, placing a hand on my shoulder. "What happened…?"

By the time I'd unloaded the story of the moose, the wolf tracks and someone watching me, Dad's face looked stern and thoughtful. He glanced around nervously.

"I'm grateful you didn't get hurt, Tater."

"Me too. Something must have scared him. It was a miracle."

"I believe so, son. We better keep our eyes out for those wolves. Keep in sight. I don't trust 'em."

"Who do you think it was?" I asked.

"The one in red?"

"Yeah, I didn't see who they were, just a glimpse."

"Well… Doesn't sound like Jasper's deerhide jacket. Not something a bow hunter would wear, either."

"Reckon it's the Bogsleys?" I asked.

I wished I could have stopped the question before it left my mouth.

Dad looked at me, his brow furrowed. "Why the Bogsleys? You okay, son?"

"I'm fine. Keep thinking they're going to steal our spot."

"What's gotten into that head of yours?"

"Ah, I don't know…" I said, kicking at the dirt.

"Well?"

"They heard I'd spotted the Old Muley. I think they're going to get to him first. They'll probably cheat and do whatever it takes."

"Hang in there, son; don't be worrying yourself about the Bogsleys. You just do your best and don't quit. Fear is a master you do not want."

I nodded.

Dad pulled my bow out of the brush and picked strands of grass and twigs from the cam-rollers and drawstring. "I was just on my way to get you when you came barreling over that hill. Carter shot a three-point buck—nice one, too! Sam sent Brock to give us word. They're dressing him out now."

"Really? Where'd he get him?"

"Sounds like Carter found a spring down in a ravine and the buck came in on him."

"Where's Brock now?"

"He went back to help while I came to find you."

✳   ✳   ✳

We soon met Sam, Brock, and Carter on the trail. Their foreheads were beaded with sweat and they were breathing hard. The hind and front quarters of the mule deer buck stuck out from their heavily loaded packs. Carter had the rack strapped to the back of his, with three long antler tines on each side. As he saw me, a smile beamed across his face.

"Sorry I missed it," I said. "I wish I was there."

"I wondered how you were doing," Carter replied. "See anything?"

"No, but a moose about ate me."

"Really?"

"Well, almost."

"Anything else?"

"No, just some wolf tracks."

"Interesting," Sam said. "I ran across tracks as well. Looks like there's a pack of them around here. We better keep on the lookout and hightail it out. Stuck out here in the dark, with meat loaded in our backpacks, is no place to be. May as well be ringing a dinner bell for those wolves."

On our way back, Carter told me all about how he had gotten the buck. He sure made it sound easy. The deer just walked into the spring and drank. Carter was downwind, hiding behind a large rock. The buck never saw it coming. Jealousy crept in the more he talked. I didn't like how it felt. It made me angry at Carter's success, though I knew I should be happy for him.

I also felt increased anxiety as my confidence in shooting a buck continued to break down. The burden of my bet for Bandit's freedom to improve my own increased in weight with every failed attempt, and the dream of ever getting the Ghost Deer felt like a distant memory.

Later, I had an idea. "Can I hunt that spot tomorrow?" I asked.

"Nah," Carter said.

"Why not? You've already filled your tag!"

"Wouldn't be any good. With the wolves in the area, they'll find the carcass. Once their scent is around the spring, no deer is coming into that hole for a while."

He had a point, and I didn't like it. With fishing, it was different. If my dad found a good hole, often he would let me try it out. I guess the fish didn't know their cousins were getting pulled out of the same spot.

After mulling this over, I asked, "So, where are we going to hunt tomorrow?"

Grinning, Sam said, "I found a spot that looks good. Believe I saw the Ghost Deer you've been talking about."

"You saw him!?"

"I'm certain it was him. Must've been at least 800 yards away, but I saw something big and white heading up a steep ravine. Place looks like the backbone of a massive dinosaur or something... it's got these tall granite spines on each side. It's by the back of the cliffs, quite a hike from where we parked.

"Even at that distance, I could tell the buck had antlers—massive ones too! I about dropped my scope when I found him again. Even had to clean off the lenses to be certain I wasn't hallucinating. You weren't kidding! I've seen a lot of big bucks in my time, but nothing like him!"

"You say by the cliffs?" I asked.

"Yep."

"What about Jasper's warning?"

"I thought about that," Sam replied, wiping sweat from his forehead. "He didn't give us much detail. Jasper's hiding something alright. Don't know about you—but I'm not afraid.

165

I'll chase the Old Muley through a den of mountain lions if I have to."

"I reckon you're right," I said. "Once you see him, he's mighty tough to get out of your head."

Soon, we spotted the trucks in our flashlights. "There's Old Brown," Grandpa said. "Let's get this meat back to camp and into the coolers. My sleeping bag's going to look like a pile of cotton clouds. I'll be sawing logs before my head hits the pillow."

The moon was now above the eastern ridge as darkness filled the high mountain basin. As the creaking door of the old Ford closed, a wolf's howl pierced the night air, and I got a chill as that eerie sense of being watched flooded back.

CHAPTER 19
DREAMS

I awoke in a cold sweat to the sounds of thunder and rain pelting the side of the trailer. Wind hissed through the seams of the window as I shifted deeper into my sleeping bag.

Despite the storm, I was glad to be awake, at least for the moment. I reached over to the counter and picked up the alarm.

"2:43 am," I muttered.

I let my head drop back onto the pillow, wiping cold beads of sweat from my forehead.

"Glad it was only a dream," I whispered.

My mind still flashed with images of gray fur and long, dagger-like fangs dripping with saliva. The tracks and the wolf's howl the day before haunted me. No one wants to feel like they're being hunted while they themselves are hunting—yet I did.

The only wolves I had ever seen in the wild were in the foothills above the ranch, a good distance away. Last year, during our annual cattle roundup, we found one of our heifers—or at least what they'd left of her. The tracks were just like those I had seen by the stream.

The same ones? I wondered.

I'd heard wolves traveled long distances, but we were near thirty miles away from home, so I shook off the idea.

I closed my eyes, attempting to regain sleep without success. Grandpa and Dad seemed to be in a snoring contest—one going, then the other. Lightning flashed through the curtains of the trailer, followed by another booming crack, as thunder echoed through the night air.

This isn't at all how I imagined the hunt would turn out. I sighed. *Crud...* I turned over, attempting to get comfortable. *Are we even going to hunt at all tomorrow?*

We had set the alarm to go off at 4:00 am, which gave me a lot of time to think. At this rate, we would start our hunt late in the morning, or at least wait until the rain stopped. Propping myself up, I pulled back the curtain, looking at the beads of water trickling down the window. Another lightning flash illuminated Carter's three-point buck rack, lying on the camp table.

How was it he always seemed to get a buck?

I'd missed three times now. Once at the three-point and twice with the Ghost Deer. "Three strikes, you're out," I whispered. I hoped not, but it sure felt that way. The bucks were winning, and by a large margin.

I wondered about the Ghost Deer. Jasper said the old buck had been around for many years, longer than any of us knew. I wasn't sure how long most bucks lived, but I figured it was far less. He seemed different, larger than life, I suppose.

Had he always been in these mountains?

I wished I could hear the stories rising from the dust of the many past hunts and grand adventures. *How many other hunters had trailed him? How many had fired shots?* I wondered. *I reckon only the forest can tell that story, though I sure would love to hear it...*

There's something about that which you cannot reach. It seems to call you, like a whisper in the wind, beckoning you to the unknown.

CHAPTER 20
ENEMIES

It was after 9:00 am that morning by the time we loaded the trucks and headed out of camp. The rain had stopped, but clouds covered the sky. Testing the 4-wheel drive to its limits, we forged through the muddy road, arriving at the pullout leading to the trail atop Sawtooth Mountain.

Unpacking our gear, we started our journey towards the ravine where Sam had last seen Old Muley through his spotting scope. He had since nicknamed this canyon the Spine, because of the massive rocks jutting from the ground on both sides of the ravine. Like the backbone of a monstrous dinosaur.

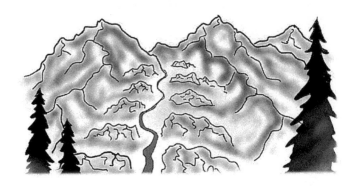

My feet felt like I had steel plates bolted to the bottom of my boots as I sloshed through the mud. It was over an hour before we reached the base of the canyon.

"What now?" I asked, staring at the jagged ravine with dread.

After the added exertion of trudging through the mud with my pack, my legs felt rubbery and my shoulders ached.

"We go up, of course," Sam said. "He's not here. Looks like nothing much is. Any tracks we see today will be fresh as of this morning."

I sighed. *After coming this far—now up?*

I wanted nothing more than to harvest the Ghost Deer, but I sure didn't want to climb the muddy mountain just to find out he wasn't there.

Grandpa pulled binoculars from his pack, scanning the trail leading to the fog-filled ravine. "There are thick patches of pine beyond the bend," he said, pointing. "It's quite a hike, but on a day like this, I suspect the deer are lying down trying to keep warm and dry."

Not a bad idea, I thought. After waking up before the alarm and not being able to fall asleep, my eyes were heavy. *Bedding down sounds good. Warm and dry—all the better.*

I tried to keep the guys from seeing my chattering teeth as I blew hot air into my cupped hands, attempting to get more movement in my fingers. In my mind, this was a man's game, and I wanted to prove I was a man.

"Tell you what," Sam said. "It won't do us any good to trudge up this ravine with the wind blowing on our backs. Any bucks bedded down up there will have all the time in the world to mosey on out."

"Brock, Carter, how about you and I hook over to the ridge up there?" he said, pointing. "We'll stay down-wind and come in on top of them, nice and slow."

Brock nodded.

Carter sighed. Since getting his buck, he seemed to have lost interest in hiking. "So—what do you say, Carter?" Sam asked, sensing his hesitation.

"Ah—alright," he said, without conviction. "You guys helped me pack my buck out. I just hope you don't get one up there," he said, chuckling. "It's going to be one heck of a hike!"

"What about us?" I asked, cutting in. "Can we go?"

"You can," Sam said. "That is, if you want to… However, I would suggest you cut around to the right and come in upwind. Hide in those boulders and brush about halfway up. It'll take some time, but when we make it around the ridge, we'll come in through those trees over there," he said, pointing. "With luck, we'll push some down to you, maybe even the old buck."

I hated to admit it, but it sounded like a good plan. And though I felt like they were getting the better end of the hunting stick, hiking to the top of the mountain didn't sound fun.

"It's settled then," Grandpa said. "Let's go."

Dad nodded in confirmation.

After a time, we made it to the selected location. Once we were there, the boulders were much larger than they looked from below. Some towered twenty to thirty feet high. Thick brush filled the spaces between them, making the going difficult.

I wish I could just jump from one boulder to the next. Man, that would be great. I feel so trapped down here in this tangled mess. I groaned, mumbling inside.

After fighting through the brush for what seemed like forever, we found a worn game trail with fresh tracks.

"I'm guessing a doe and a fawn," I said, pointing at the tracks streaking through the mud. "Looks like they slipped and slid all the way down."

Dad bent over for a closer look. "Appears that way to me," he said. "At least we know there are deer moving. That's a good sign."

We followed the trail in search of a position with a view of the ravine near the thick pines. As we came around a large boulder, I saw a single set of flared-out hoof prints crossing the trail, pressed deep into the mud. "Looks like he came through here," I said, pointing with excitement.

"Sure did," Grandpa whispered. "Fresh, too. See there? Water's still seeping into the track."

Excitement rippled through my body. Not only was he here, but he was close.

Grandpa motioned for us to gather around. Whispering, he said, "Looks like we're getting near the ravine. With the pines not far away, those boulders might be the best spot. We could use them as tree stands. Positioned high, your scent is off the ground. If you're careful, and stay low without moving, the bucks might not know you're there."

After some discussion, we spread out, placing ourselves along the ravine's edge—selecting tall, fin-shaped boulders as vantage points.

My heart pounded with anticipation as I fought for footing, driving my muddy boots into a crack to climb the massive boulder. All the while, I struggled to keep my bow slung over my shoulder. By the time I made it to the top, my knees throbbed and my hands stung.

Once on top, I crept to the edge. *Woah! Higher than I thought.* I stumbled back, attempting to catch my balance as a powerful gust of air funneled down the canyon.

I soon found a low spot on the rock and sat, only my head and shoulders exposed.

In the ravine's bottom, I spotted the main trail leading from the base, extending to the top. Though that trail was out of range, another veered off, winding through the brush to my right.

That's the one, I thought.

It looked like an escape route, and the perfect spot to make an ambush.

My stomach growled. I checked my watch: 1:35 pm. *No wonder I'm hungry.*

Still no sign of deer. I ate a peanut butter sandwich and some chips before settling back, attempting to get comfortable.

Dad and Grandpa had given me the highest spot next to the pines. I figured they were being generous, or maybe they were just sick of tramping through the brush. Either way, I was grateful to have what I considered the best location.

I looked over in Dad's direction, scanning the boulder he'd selected about 150 yards away. I spotted him moving into position on the rock. "There he is," I whispered. *I wonder if he can see me,* I thought as I settled in, attempting to hide from the cool breeze.

Squirrels chattered in the nearby forest. *They sure are noisy little creatures, always yip yapping at anything passing by.* I yawned and stretched as I attempted to get comfortable. *I guess it's alright—helps me not feel so alone.*

A breeze rustled through the trees. I pulled my jacket tighter. With the humid air, my thermal underwear and outer clothing weren't doing a bit of good. *I wish those darn bushes below were up here on this rock,* I thought. *Sure could use some cover.*

My excitement and anticipation soon drained, when all I saw minute after minute were the same empty trails and boring trees as the rock dug into my rear end and back.

I wonder if Sam and the guys are having any luck? Where are all those deer they're supposed to be pushing down, anyway? At this rate, it could be hours. I sighed, playing with the zipper on my backpack. *I guess they do have one heck of a hike... Probably will stop for breaks along the way.*

I dreamed and strategized until my eyes grew heavy. All the while, the rhythmic sounds of the wind droned on, playing a soft lullaby through the tall pines.

I wish I wasn't so hard on Molly for wanting to come hunting next year. My sister was a tomboy at heart and the closest thing to a brother I had. *I wonder how she'll handle it.* I thought. The hunt hadn't been easy, and if I weren't trying to prove that I was a man, I dare say I would've complained much more.

I thought about Parley Bogsley. As little kids, we had been good friends.

It's been a long time... I thought.

That was before Parley's dad got hurt in the farming accident, and his mom left. In the years after, Parley just kept getting sorer and meaner every year, until about three years ago we had a big falling out.

My mind drifted back to that time in fourth grade on the school playground. I adjusted my jacket tighter and lay back, glaring at the cloud-filled sky. I hoped to see some sign of blue. *Nothing!* My eyes drooped, my rock bed becoming increasingly comfortable until my world went black.

*　　*　　*

"Molly Polly braided hair. You look like a horse from way up here," Parley said, sitting atop the monkey bars and glaring down at Molly.

She kept rocking back and forth, talking to her friend in the next swing over.

"Hey Molly! I'm talking to you. You think you're too good for me?"

Molly looked up at him and stuck out her tongue. From over on the slide where I sat, I saw Parley drop to the ground, walking in Molly's direction. Halfway down the tube slide, I heard a scream. As I shot out the end, I turned to see Parley yank down on Molly's braid.

"Leave me alone!" she yelled, trying to kick back at him with her foot.

"Ah, you're just a tomboy," Parley said. "You're no girl in those overalls... Why ain't you wearing something pretty and pink like Sally over there?" he asked, pointing.

Molly's lip quivered. "I am too a girl! Let go of my hair."

179

"Why, tomboy? You going to make me?"

"You leave her alone!" I called out, charging over.

Parley let go of her braid. "Oh, now look here, your big brother coming to save you. How sweet."

"You apologize, or you're going to have to answer to me."

"Oh, big talker, are ya? Seems to me you're just a runt yourself. I don't think you've got it in ya."

Parley shoved Molly, causing her to stumble into the playground gravel. She looked at her hands and cried.

"That's it, Parley! You leave her alone! I don't want to see you touch her ever again!"

"Why should I? You're my friend, aren't ya?"

"Not anymore, Parley! If you're going to treat Molly that way, you're no friend of mine!"

I ducked my head and charged, throwing my full weight into his chest. Pain blazed through my shoulder as our bodies collided. I shot out my arms to break my fall, digging them deep into the gravel.

My hands and knees felt raw. Parley got up and spun on top of me, shoving my face into the rock-filled dirt. He pulled my hair and I cried out in pain, twisting onto my back. Punching hard, I beat on both sides of his ribs like an angry gorilla. Parley exhaled, gasping for breath. Rolling off, he attempted to get out of range.

Then, a large hand picked me up from the back of my overalls. "No fighting, boys!" Mr. Porter said sternly. "What's this all about?"

He had Parley gripped by the shoulder in his other hand, and we glared at each other with wild fury.

"Some friend!" I said.

Parley spat. "What friend? You ain't no friend of mine!"

CHAPTER 21
SHOWDOWN

I must have fallen asleep, for I awakened with a start to the sound of thumping hooves and rustling brush. Disoriented, I searched for my bow, snatching it up. I nocked an arrow.

I peered above the rock. Two bucks were coming up the side trail leading from the ravine. My hands shook as I slid my fingers over my bowstring.

Submerged in the tall undergrowth, it was difficult to see. But what I saw was enough—head, neck, and antlers!

The first buck was a nice four-point mule deer, not a monster, but respectable, sporting long tines and a spread just past his ears. Trailing about twenty yards behind was a two-point buck, smaller in body, with a second-year rack, two large forks on each side.

The bucks bounded along the trail, as if running from something. The guys above must have spooked them. I stood slowly, remaining in a crouch. *Just breathe*, I scolded myself. *Take your time...*

The four-point let out a loud snort, bounding over a log lying across the trail.

If I pull back my bow now, they might not see me, but can I hold the draw?

The sound of hooves cracking on the rock grew louder. Sweat slithered down the side of my head into my ear. It tickled. I desperately wanted to wipe it out, but I couldn't take the risk.

Hold until they're closer... But, if I wait, I'll have only seconds to take the shot. I cussed myself inside, scrambling for a solution.

The bigger buck's black eyes and twitching nose scanned for danger. I ducked lower, afraid he might see me. I attempted to draw my bow from a kneeling position, trying to remain concealed. I soon realized my error. Not only could I no longer see the buck, but unbearable pain shot through my knees as they dug into the coarse rock.

Bracing my hand, I shoved off the boulder and stood. The buck was now moving along the trail in front of me. A thousand different scenarios flashed through my mind. What to do, and how to do it… all the hunting videos I had watched and all the stories meant nothing now.

They're not the Ghost Deer, but these are good bucks, and the first one's even bigger than Carter's. Will I get this chance again? I wondered. "What about the Ghost Deer?" I whispered. *Is it failure not to hold out for him?*

Uncle Sam's words came to mind. *'Tater, what makes you think success is only bringing home Old Muley?'*

What to do?

Then I remembered Bandit. It was as if he were sitting right beside me, with those soft black eyes looking up. I shook my head, releasing the image.

The buck bounded down the trail to my right. My hand shook as I raised my bow and pulled back. The four-point instantly spotted me, dug in his hooves, and jerked his head back as my arrow spiraled towards him. Lunging forward, he dipped low and the broadhead collided with a rock, flipping into the air.

"Ahh man! ... No!" I hissed.

I hadn't accounted for either the buck dipping or my overhead position. The arrow went right over his back. The four-point bounded down the trail even as I grabbed another arrow, letting it fly. It drove into the dirt behind him. Snatching another, I nocked it and pulled back, scanning for the two-point. I spotted him thirty yards away, facing me. He looked side to side as if trying to figure out which way to run.

"Now or never!" I whispered.

I aimed lower, this time releasing the arrow towards his chest. As it flew, a breeze fishtailed it to the right, causing it to penetrate his upper leg. He reared back, turning away from the trail and bounded into the brush.

I shot again—this time, with the buck sixty yards away. I saw the fletching vibrate as the arrow struck a large pine. At the same moment, the buck darted past.

"Nooooo!" I cried out. "I just wounded him! I should have waited… I should have waited!"

I felt horrible. I had always wanted to make a clean kill. I had practiced so long for this very day.

I grabbed my gear and threw on my pack. *He can't go far… With some luck, I'll find him. I've got to!*

My breath heavy, I slid down the rock, leaping to the ground.

I can't let him get away!

Grabbing my arrow from the trail, I cut through the brush. Without a path, the going was slow through the tangled mess. Sweat poured into my eyes and branches tore at my face and arms.

Ouch! That buck made it look easy!

After several valuable minutes, I broke through to the other side, running uphill towards my arrow stuck in the pine, the last place I'd seen the buck. Bending low, I scanned for any sign of blood. Five yards away, I found a branch marked red.

I soon located his tracks as I plunged deeper into the forest. A loud crack echoed through the trees. I searched the scattered pines and brush ahead, running, searching, and waiting. With every moving branch or rustle of leaves, my eyes found something that looked like a buck, only to vanish in an instant. Another branch broke, this time farther away.

The thick trees limited my visibility. *Man, all this grass and plant life is making trailing difficult. How am I supposed to find a track?* The air felt moist and smelled of damp wood and soil. A quiet rumbling rolled through the mountains as thunder approached.

It was then I found a broken twig and a drop of blood on a nearby leaf.

Good! Still have the trail.

The sounds of breaking branches and thumping hooves grew faint. Coughing from lack of breath, I hunched over, gripping my knees for support. "I'm losing him!" I whispered. "I can't! I just can't!"

The trail was getting harder to follow, the signs of his passing becoming more spread out and difficult to find. *I should have waited when I first shot the buck,* I scolded myself.

He might have bedded down. Now who knows how far he's going to run?

I found a trail heading in the general direction, with fresh deer droppings. Desperate, I ran. All the pain and all the regret of wounding an animal I would likely never find tormented me. My best friend, my dog, almost surely lost now to the Bogsleys. *Why did I hurry so fast? Why did I think I could do something so hard?* I kicked myself inside, over and over. Reed's words filled my mind with driving force, like punches to the gut. *'You don't have any idea what you're getting into, expecting to bring home a buck on your first-year archery hunt... Hah!'*

My panting breath and plodding feet paled compared to the agony I felt inside. My lungs were ready to burst, aching and searing with pain. Mixed emotion filled me, battling for control of my thoughts. Excited at having shot my first buck— yet focused on my responsibility to find him and end his suffering.

No, it hadn't gone as I had hoped. If it had, I would be by the boulder right now with my buck. I was on a mission, and honor and commitment were far greater motivators.

Sweat stung my eyes, blurring my vision. Greens and browns flashed through my view as I charged into the thick forest.

Suddenly, I caught movement to my right, large and white. Skidding, I stopped. Only twenty yards away, standing broadside in the trees, was the Ghost Deer!

I froze, not flinching a muscle. His blue eyes and silvery white coat glistened, despite the darkness of the cloud-covered sky. He snorted with power, dipping his head in acknowledgement of my presence.

Four arrows remained in my quiver.

If I'm careful, I might get a shot. Dad will give me his tag—won't he? I'm probably not even going to find the two-point again. No one even knows... I've done my best. This is my chance. This is Bandit's freedom!

As the massive buck turned to face me, the muscles rippled in his neck. Mist barreled from his nostrils as he exhaled deep breaths of warm air. The buck's head tilted, as if inquiring my thoughts.

My hand crawled towards my quiver. The buck snorted, pawing the ground with his front hoof and shaking his head.

My heartbeat increased, thudding against my rib cage like a war drum, increasing in intensity. I exhaled, slow and deliberate. His rack was unbelievable, a spiderweb of antlers, as if formed by the union of many bucks. The King of the Forest—this was his domain, his fortress.

The Ghost Deer's eyes pierced mine. I reached for an arrow. Three were missing, a reminder of a buck forgotten. Temptation drove me further.

I'll show those Bogsleys! This is for freedom.

I grabbed the nearest one and nocked it on my bowstring with care.

Inside, the battle raged on. *I've already shot my buck! I saw the arrow and I've seen the blood. Will I ever find him? Not a chance... but our freedom is on the line. How can I not?*

My whole body shook with adrenaline as I gripped the string tighter, the muscles in my forearm straining as I drew back. The buck's eyes narrowed, his gaze fixed.

Silence fell over the forest. My beating heart and soft breath were the only sounds. I adjusted my stance and felt a bead of sweat crawling down the side of my face. The muscles in my arm and shoulder burned against the resistance of the tensioned string.

The buck's eyes locked on mine, just as my twenty-yard sight pin found its place on Old Muley's chest.

Steady now—steady.

Everything in my body wanted to let go of the string, and everything in my mind justified it.

All I have to do is let go.

I had practiced this shot a thousand times. It would find its mark.

You've done all you could do to find the two-point. I shook my head, attempting to remove the tormenting thought.

Have I?

The question plagued my mind. The Ghost Deer snorted, dipping his head to reveal countless points from a new angle. My breath stopped.

Why is he not running? Why is he not fighting?

I had seen what he could do when pressed. Yet, he seemed to wait.

But for what? A decision? Yes—my decision.

I knew then what I had to do. And though everything in my mind said *Shoot!* Everything inside me said *No!*

With renewed determination, I lowered my bow. This was not the time or the place. There was a buck out there, my buck. I had a duty to honor the life he would give. The Ghost Deer nodded, as if acknowledging my decision. Then, with an echoing snort, he leaped high in the air, landing twenty feet away as he bounded into the depths of the forest.

A wolf howled in the distance. "My buck!" I yelled. "They're after my buck!"

CHAPTER 22

THE LAST STAND

The wolf's howl came from the north, deep in the thick pines. A loud clap of thunder startled me as I scanned the area, attempting to pinpoint the pack's location. Another *"Boom!"* rattled through the darkening clouds churning above. I looked back at the trail with longing. The trailer and the warmth of a fire called to me, pulling with unseen strength. Turning, I listened again for the wolves. Another howl rang through the forest, this time closer.

Light rain pattered against the vegetation. The wind picked up, rustling the quaking aspens on the edge of the meadow. "Crud!" I said, adjusting my slumping backpack. I questioned whether I should hightail it out and attempt to find my way back. The storm was fast approaching. In my experience helping Dad on cattle drives, I knew the mountain rains were relentless. Despite this, I had wounded a buck, and the wolves were on his trail.

I cupped my hands around my mouth and yelled, "Dad!" Pausing, I listened for an answer. "Grandpa! ... Can you hear me? I'm back here!"

I doubted they had seen me shoot the buck or climb off the boulder. I was in it deep, way over my head, without even realizing it was happening. Suddenly, a terrifying feeling of being lost and alone came on me with striking force. Lightning flashed, and a clap of thunder echoed along the cliffs.

My heart rate increased. I eyed the tree line to the north and took in a deep draw of air, filling my lungs. Exhaling slowly, I gripped my bow tighter.

I had the choice to fight—or to run. I knew the wolves would outnumber me. Yet if I ran, not only would I give up my first buck, but choosing to shrink in the face of fear would haunt me with guilt like a shadow.

Why fight anyway? It's just a buck… there will be more. He's a nice two-point, but worth risking my life for?

I had quit on goals before, more than I would like to admit. Despite this, hitting the buck in the front foreleg plagued me. If I didn't finish what I had set out to do, he would suffer.

All because of my poor shot!

This felt heavy, a burden I hadn't expected to receive.

I hate the thought of the wolves taking him. Without his injury, he may have outrun them, but not now.

The tall lodgepole pines and subalpine firs made an impenetrable wall. Focused on trailing the buck, I hadn't looked for landmarks or flagged a return path. I was at least a mile in and lost.

"Dad! Are you there?" I yelled. The only response was the rhythmic sounds of pattering rain.

I had never felt so alone and conflicted. If I tried to go back, I might get turned around and more lost than ever. Another wolf's howl rang out, cut short by a clap of thunder.

What about Bandit? Would I abandon him?

Dad and Mom had taught me about character my whole life, but it wasn't until now that I understood what it meant. I took a deep breath, turning in the sound's direction.

"Not today, Scar Face. Get your own buck!" I said as I straightened the brim of my hat.

At a dead run, I drove into the thick subalpine firs at the edge of the meadow. Branches clawed at my clothes and hands as I dodged the towering trees, leaping over fallen logs and brush. Another howl, this time to my right.

They're moving—and fast.

Soon I came to a steep hill, littered with thick dogwood and scattered willows leading to a river in the base of a ravine. My hopes sank.

"No! Not now!" I yelled, kicking at the thick undergrowth.

Sighing, I held my bow overhead, wading through the brush. Searching for footing, I plowed into the entangled barricade blocking my path. It felt as if bobcats were clawing at my legs, yet I couldn't stop. *There's only one way out of this mess*—and that's *forward*.

Images of my buck running from the wolves filled my imagination. I quickened my pace. After a few steps, I stumbled, falling forward. A branch caught my cheek, accompanied by a sharp burning pain, as I crashed into the dense undergrowth.

"Aaahhh!" I cried out.

As I struggled to get up, the entwined branches pulled me back. The sprinkling rain increased to a steady drizzle as I lay buried in the sea of leaves. I wanted to hide. I wanted to give up. I wanted to go home.

Images of the two-point flashed through my mind. I replayed the poor shot over and over, lying in the damp branches and leaves—wet and alone. Guilt seeped in deeper than rain.

He'll suffer because of my choice. I need to make this right.

Frantically, I unclipped the chest strap on my pack. Once free, I worked it loose. I found my bow nestled in the brush and yanked. A branch snapped, releasing it. With my pack and bow high above my head, I fought through branch by branch, step by step. After a few minutes, I arrived at the river's edge as the dense undergrowth opened up into a patch of tall grass.

Rain dripped from my camo ball cap, and steam rose from my sweat-riddled body. I tightened my jaw, trying to ignore the burning pain radiating from the scratches along my arms and legs as I scanned for options.

The river's current was swift, the water level rising. Downstream, more howls sounded above the raging water. Desperate, I frantically searched for a way to cross—a fallen log, something—anything would do.

I found a sturdy branch and kicked off the limbs, making a staff. I looped the tie-down straps on my backpack around my bow and cinched them tight, adjusting the four remaining broadheads, securing them in the quiver. I put the pack on and clipped in the chest strap, huffing out a chest full of air. Turning to face the river, I sucked in a deep breath, gripped the staff with both hands, and raced forward, leaping high into the air.

The long limb dug deep into the water, dropping lower than I expected, throwing me off balance. Instead of using the pole to vault over the river, I fell forward. Sharp pain shot through my shoulder as it collided with the staff. There was a loud *"snap!"* and in an instant, a million cold needles shot through my body, crushing the air from my lungs.

As I exhaled into the biting blanket of water, my knee collided with a rock, spinning me forward. I kicked out. Finding footing, I shoved off, launching upward.

Gasping for air, I fought to keep my head above water. Through clouded eyes, I searched for a branch to latch hold of. My hand caught something prickly and rough. I gripped it tight. My body rose to the surface, the current attempting to tear my grip free. Water flooded over my face as I strained to keep hold. Struggling to breathe, I lost my grip; the river pulled me downstream.

The churning water held me prisoner in its powerful current for a couple hundred yards before slowing into a deep pool. Heavy with water, the weight of my pack pulled me under.

My feet hit the bottom. Unclipping the pack, I yanked and pulled, attempting to peel its weight from my shoulders. Once free, I searched through the bubbling blackness for my bow, finding it still tied to the straps. I jerked at the wet knots holding it. My lungs burned for want of air as sticks and debris swirled around me. A fish swam by, brushing my neck, sending a jolt of fear through my body.

Grabbing my bow, I ripped it free from the pack. As I broke the surface, I fought against the weight of my wet boots and clothing, swimming frantically for shore. Within moments, my feet found footing.

I stumbled from the river, collapsing onto the rain-soaked grass, coughing out water. Shivering uncontrollably, I attempted to stand, slipping back onto my knees in the mud. In desperation, I turned to the only one who knew where I was. "God, please help me!" I pleaded, looking at the dark clouds above. "Please don't let me die! I don't know what to do."

Rain poured down around me, splashing up from puddles in the surrounding mud. Using my bow for support, I regained my feet, breathing heavy. Loud howls sounded in the nearby forest. I looked around, frantic, searching for a place to hide. *"Snap! Crack!"* The sounds of breaking branches increased, quickly growing louder. *"Snap! Crack! Howl..."*

"They're here," I whispered.

Adrenaline surged through my body. My hand shook as I pulled an arrow from my quiver, nocking it on the string. Loud cracks of splintering branches sounded in the pines ahead.

It felt as if my ribs would break and my heart would explode. *"Snap! Crack! Thump, thump... howl!"* I drew back my bow, straining against the numbness in my arms.

Aiming toward the oncoming fury, I whispered, "Steady now—steady." I drew in a deep breath, exhaled, and attempted to calm my wavering aim.

"Thump, thump, crack!" The two-point buck burst from the tree line only thirty feet away, heading straight for me, limping heavily on one side with the arrow still in his

foreleg. He snorted, shaking his head as he bolted forward, wild-eyed and breathing heavy.

My buck!

The string slid from my fingers and the arrow blazed through the air, striking the deer's chest.

As it penetrated, he fell, flipping towards me. Before I had time to react, the back end of the buck rammed into my legs, launching me. I landed on my back with a sharp thud, which knocked the air from my lungs. Pain shot through my body and I tasted blood. My world spun as I rolled several times before splashing into the edge of the river.

My buck was down, but so was I.

Where's my blasted bow!?

With my arms wrapped around my aching chest, I gasped for air forcing myself to get up.

A massive gray wolf, which had to be Scar Face, emerged from the tree line, followed by his pack. Fangs exposed, he growled, deep and rumbling, piercing me with his yellow eyes. Lightning flashed overhead, and a low roar of thunder rolled across the high mountain pass.

I spotted my bow, lying half covered in the tall grass. I struggled to catch my breath as I staggered from the edge of the pool and fell towards my only hope of survival. The wolves neared, saliva dripping from their open mouths.

I crawled the remaining distance, grabbed my bow, and rose to my knees. A white wolf charged from the side. Frantically, I yanked an arrow from the quiver. Nocking it, I turned and shot. The wolf yelped, falling to the ground as the broadhead met its mark.

Another lunged forward.

I didn't have time to aim, and my second shot missed the side of its head, glancing off a tree. The wolf charged towards me, his eyes narrowed and fangs ready to bite.

Without time to react, I yanked another arrow from my quiver, rolled onto my back, and thrust it upward.

The sharp broadhead blades met the wolf's neck just as its jaw brushed past my face and snapped shut. The animal fell on top of me, its warm weight crushing the air from my lungs as the musty odor of wild wet dog filled my nostrils. With all the strength I had, I pushed the lifeless creature off, rolling to my side.

I attempted to get up and slipped. Once again, pain shot through my already aching chest as it collided with the muddy ground. Rain pelted my soaked body, surrounding me in a cold, wet blanket I couldn't remove. More lightning flashed, and thunder echoed along the surrounding cliffs.

Scar Face, the massive gray wolf with a jagged scar across his eye, was now steps away. He revealed his razor-sharp teeth, smiling with evil in his eyes. As if saying, *"I have won. You simple, insignificant creature."*

His dangling tongue lapped at the saliva drizzling from his mouth, his eyes cold and lifeless. Scar Face lifted his head towards the darkened sky and howled in victory, sending spider-like sensations crawling down my neck.

Shoving myself to my knees, I lunged to the side, grabbing my last arrow. As I did, Scar Face sunk his teeth into my arm. I cried out in pain and jerked back, releasing my only hope of defense. I fought to pull free, losing my balance and landing on my back.

His large yellow eyes narrowed as saliva dripped onto my face, the scar burning into my memory like a dagger. I swung my other arm around, bringing it down hard on his nose.

"Let go!"

Scar Face snarled, jerking back, tightening his jaws. Piercing pain burned through my forearm. Fear washed over me at the sudden realization that this was my last stand. It was impossible. His strength and size far exceeded my own.

"Help!" I cried out. "Someone help!"

I felt hopeless and alone. I had known this battle would be hard, but I hadn't thought that to save my dog's life, I would have to give my own.

Just then, a loud snort echoed through the river bottom, followed by a *"thump, thump, thump!"* As I looked up, I saw the Ghost Deer flying overhead, spraying mud as he landed in the middle of the pack. *"Snort! Snort!"* He stamped his front hooves, planting them deep into the mud. Shaking his massive rack of antlers, he squared his shoulders, extending a challenge to the wolves.

Scar Face released my arm, snarling as if to say, *"I'll be back,"* then whipped around to face the narrow, piercing eyes of Old Muley.

Steam poured from the massive buck's nostrils as the pack circled their prey.

A wolf lunged. The buck spun around, catching him with his rack in midair. There was a sound of cracking bone and the wolf howled in pain, sliding into the grass fifteen feet away—motionless.

Another wolf darted in for the buck's back leg. The Ghost Deer kicked his hoof, catching the wolf on the jaw, sending him rolling backwards.

The pack's circle expanded as more wolves joined, funneling in from the trees. Scar Face stretched his neck high and howled. Together, the pack joined him in an eerie melody of song as they finished surrounding the massive buck.

Outnumbered, at least ten to one, Old Muley stood his ground.

I fought to get up. "Noooo! Leave him alone! It's me you want! I took your buck!"

Three more wolves leaped from the side.

Thrashing his head, the great white buck swept through them like a bat hitting a ball. The wolves spun through the air, landing on two of their companions who yelped out in pain.

Scar Face lunged, attempting to take the Ghost Deer from behind.

"No!" I yelled, searching for my last arrow in the churned mud.

Without warning, the buck jumped, twisting his body around, landing behind the gray wolf. Mud sprayed across my face.

Scar Face whirled around in surprise, snapping and snarling. The rest of the pack backed away as their giant alpha faced off against the King of the Forest.

The monstrous wolf revealed his long, dagger-like teeth. He growled deep and low, his fur bristling. Old Muley stomped his hooves, ripping out mud. He snorted, dipping his head as he prepared for the assault.

Scar Face circled, looking for a window of opportunity. A wolf darted in from the back, going for Old Muley's hind leg. The massive buck kicked high in the air. In this moment of distraction, Scar Face lunged forward, going for the Ghost Deer's throat.

The buck slammed his back hooves down on top of the unsuspecting wolf coming in from behind, smashing him into the mud. With lighting speed, the Ghost Deer spun around, dodging as the jaws of Scar Face snapped closed—just missing.

The muscles in the buck's neck rippled as he twisted, scooping up the off-balanced Scar Face with his brush-like antlers and lifting him high over his head.

With a loud snort, the Ghost Deer thrust his neck forward, throwing Scar Face into the air. The wolf's legs thrashed for balance for a few seconds before landed in the river with a splash.

The buck snorted, spinning around, eyeing the remaining pack. Whimpering, they backed up, fear filling their eyes.

On the far side of the river, Scar Face crawled from the water, limping. He shook off his wet coat, turned and howled, low and sorrowful. The pack shifted, circling the buck. They broke into a run, jumped into the pool, and swam the remaining distance. Once on the other side, they followed their defeated leader, slinking out of sight.

The Ghost Deer turned to face me.

Should I run? Aren't I his enemy too?

His breath was soft, his blue eyes inquiring.

"Thank—you," I whispered, extending my hand and struggling to regain my feet. "I owe you my life. Please—please don't hurt me..." I said, stammering, extending both hands and backing away.

He snorted, dipping his head. I took another couple of steps, hands outstretched, as I scanned for an escape route. Old Muley stared at me with those big blue eyes, breathing heavy. He then nodded, snorted softly and turned, bounding off into the cover of the pines as quickly as he had come.

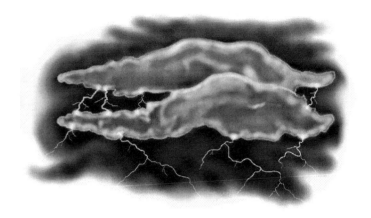

CHAPTER 23

THE STORM

Left alone in the gathering darkness and rain, my teeth chattered. *Why did Old Muley save me?* I questioned, wrapping my arms around my chest. *He ought to have thrown me into the river right alongside Scar Face. Has he forgotten my arrows?*

I wondered how long the buck had lived, and all he had experienced. Maybe someone had saved his life once, and he was paying the gift forward. Whatever his reasons were, I was grateful, and I considered it an answer to my prayer. God was aware of me. Of this, I was certain. And despite my many weaknesses, he cared enough to hear my pleadings—an alone boy, on a lost and forgotten mountain.

I did my best to steady myself. My head was spinning with exhaustion; never had I felt so beaten up and frozen as I did now.

After retrieving my compound bow, I combed through the mud with my fingers until finding my last arrow. I walked over to the buck, who lay motionless. With two large forks on each side, he was a respectable first buck.

Gratitude filled me for the life he had given.

Wet to the bone, I desperately wanted to get out of the rain. Yet, having lost my pack to the river, I no longer had a way to make a fire and get warm. Kneeling, I admired the mule deer's sleekness and beauty. I placed my hand on his coat and was surprised to find he was still warm. This gave me an idea.

I soon found a large pine with a thick bed of dry needles around its base, at the edge of the meadow. I left my bow and went back for the buck.

Gripping his front hooves with both hands, I pulled hard. He didn't move. Though small compared to the larger bucks I had seen, he was much heavier than expected—weighing more than myself.

I tried again, this time with all the strength I had. The buck slid a couple of inches through the wet grass before my grip failed, landing me in the mud. I tried once more, with the same result.

"At this rate, it'll take hours to get the buck back to the tree," I said weakly.

As I returned to the river, I scanned the pool for any signs of my pack. I knew I had to search the bottom, though it was the last thing I wanted to do. I went to take my hat off, then realized it wasn't there. "Must've lost it in the river," I mumbled. Wading into the pool, I headed for the center, where I remembered last having it.

I dove under, finding nothing but mud and rock squishing through my fingers. I plunged into the water again, searching longer with the same result.

Feelings of desperation came. I started bobbing under repeatedly, probing with my feet, scanning small sections. Within minutes, my foot hooked onto something different. I dove once more, searching the icy darkness. I soon grabbed the strap of my pack, feeling the woven fibers covered in mud.

I pulled it on shore, dumped out the water and found my food ruined except for a wrapped candy bar. My canteen was still half full, for which I was grateful, yet my matches were as wet as an otter.

I took my pack to the spot I had selected and pulled out my rope. Clearing away some of the lower branches with my hatchet, I tied the rope around the trunk of the large pine before taking the other end to the buck.

Cutting off a two-foot length, I lashed the front legs of the buck together, checking its hold. I then looped the end of the rope tied to the tree around the lashings between the buck's hooves, using the lashings as a pulley. This increased my leverage. It was hard, but by pulling on the end of the rope, I dragged the buck to the tree in fifteen minutes.

Once there, I struggled to catch my breath, then dragged him the remaining distance under the tree by hand, tugging and pulling at the lashings. My teeth no longer chattered uncontrollably, though my mind felt foggy. Though I was warmed by my exertions, I knew that wouldn't last. I had heard of hypothermia, but had never been cold enough to experience it. Wet, without a sleeping bag or fire, I was at risk of freezing during the night.

With the buck in position, I curled up with my back next to him. He was still warm, but his heat was fading.

Rain pattered in the forest, dripping from the pine tree like an umbrella. The tall aspens and pines groaned in protest to the roaring wind. Burrowing deeper into the thick bed of pine needles, I attempted to find relief from its bite.

Soon after settling in, I noticed a throbbing pain in my right forearm. I rolled back my sleeve and saw the punctures where Scar Face's fangs had penetrated.

Fortunately, the bleeding had stopped. Without even realizing it, I had washed my wounds in the river while looking for my backpack. I unzipped the front pocket, finding my first aid kit. After applying antiseptic, I wrapped my arm with gauze, securing it in place as best I could.

I settled back in against the buck. He had a strong gamey odor, but I didn't care, grateful he gave his life to save mine.

I munched on my Snickers bar in silence as I listened to the fury of the storm, wondering if Dad and the guys would be okay. I didn't know how to find them and prayed they would find me. With the oncoming night and dropping temperatures, my only hope of survival was staying out of the rain and finding warmth.

Scooping armfuls of pine needles, I covered my exposed body with their insulating blanket. *I sure wish I'd brought a flint and steel,* I thought, slapping the ground with my hand. Regret filled my mind as I agonized at my forgetfulness. *My raincoat won't do me any good drying out at camp.*

Never had I been in a situation so relentless, life-threatening, and out of my control. Filled with thoughts of family and home, I wrapped my arms around my chest as my heavy eyes settled into a world of black stillness.

CHAPTER 24
THE RESCUE

When I awoke, I felt warm. I tried to move, but my legs felt stuck. Blackness filled my view. Along with the rustling of trees, there were sounds that did not belong. I heard deep breathing in front of me. As I strained to roll over, my face brushed up against something hairlike.

Fur? Can't be...

I rocked back and forth attempting to move again. I was trapped—wedged between my two-point buck and something warm and soft in front of me. I lay motionless.

What is this?

In the darkness, it appeared gray.

An animal, perhaps? Does it realize I'm here?

My left arm lay underneath me, numb with limited circulation. I had to get up, at least reposition.

The last thing I need is a wolf or bear realizing I'm right behind them.

I felt like a prisoner in my body.

How long will this last? I wondered.

Whatever it was, it was very large, blocking all view of the surrounding forest. I was grateful to still be alive and warm. But I wondered if I would remain that way for long.

The creature shifted.

What will I do when daylight comes?

My bandaged arm ached, throbbing in pain. I wasn't sure I could last until morning, not like this. Even if I did, then what? *Eaten!* My mind raced, tormented by the possibilities.

Why hadn't this animal already dragged me out from under the tree? Couldn't he smell? Was he saving me for a later meal?

The monstrous creature shifted. I held my breath, not daring to move. I shivered as an icy breeze blasted me from the front. Long muscular legs appeared, silhouetted in the moonlight. I looked up, attempting to see what it was, but pine branches blocked my view.

Mist billowed through the pine boughs and branches cracked as the creature pushed back the limbs. I attempted to scream for help but heard only a sigh of squeaky air. As the beast's head dipped under the tree, my wide eyes met the glowing gaze of Old Muley.

His beaming blue eyes narrowed, and warm mist and smells of consumed vegetation filled my nostrils. Pine branches crackled above as the Ghost Deer nuzzled his large black nose towards me.

Snorting softly, he withdrew. The massive buck stood motionless as our eyes locked. Swallowing hard, I shifted back, pressing tight against my buck. He pawed the ground with his hoof, flicked his ears and turned, lumbering off into the forest.

I lay still for several minutes after the Ghost Deer left, trying to make sense of the encounter and wondering if he would return.

How long had he been there, shielding me from the wind? And to save me—again?

I was much drier than before, and though my skin recoiled with goosebumps at the wind's bite, I felt warm inside.

Why does he even care about me? And to forgive all that I've done?

I didn't feel worthy of the gifts he had given. With an effort, I shifted off my side onto my back, allowing the blood to return to my left arm.

Tingling with needle-like sensation, it regained strength until I could move my fingers. Scooping pine needles back around me, I repositioned against my buck.

I glanced at my watch: 4:43 am. I had been out most of the night.

The wind kicked up, increasing in intensity. Dark, billowing clouds moved across the moon, covering the forest with a blanket of darkness. The trees creaked, the air smelling of moss and pine.

I wonder if there are any widow-makers nearby?

Dad taught me to always look for standing dead trees before setting up camp. At risk of blowing over in the wind, they could be death traps in a storm such as this.

I lay there for a while, attempting to stay warm in my bed of pine needles, pondering why the old buck had saved me from freezing during the night.

Jasper had called him the Guardian—hadn't he. Yes, that's it...

I chuckled. "A Guardian he is."

And a forgiver... I thought, glancing at my bow.

Just then, I heard a faint yell.

I sat up. "Dad? Is that you?"

I heard it again, this time closer. "Help! Please—someone help!" It sounded like a boy.

One of my cousins, perhaps? Did Carter get lost?

I kicked off the pine needles covering my legs before crawling out from under the tree. Rain dripped off my hair, running into my eyes. *I sure wish I hadn't lost my hat,* I thought, stretching my stiff back.

Wind howled through the groaning trees.

My eyes caught movement. A small beam of light bobbed up and down, coming closer. "Over here!" I yelled, waving my arms. I doubted they would see me, but I had to try. "It's me! Over here... It's Tate." Lightning flashed, and for an instant, I saw someone running across an opening in the pines. I clapped, yelling and whooping.

"Can you see me?"

The flashlight waved in my direction.

Without a light of my own, I crept forward, feeling with my feet and hands, attempting to find a way through the darkness.

"Hey, who's there?" the voice called out.

"It's Tate, I'm over here!" I yelled. "Is that you, Carter?"

The light was now behind the patch of trees separating me from the meadow. Soon, they made their way around a patch of pines ten yards to my right. I put up my hand, squinting as the light hit my eyes.

"Who's there?" I yelled.

"Rat! Is that you?"

My words caught in my throat. There was only one person who called me Rat—one I did not like.

"Parley! What are you doing up here?" I asked, scowling, looking around for my bow.

"Huntin, just like you. What do you think I'd be doing out in this rain?"

"I got my buck, Parley!" I said angrily, pointing in the tree's direction. "You and Reed better be leaving me and Bandit alone—we had a deal."

"Fine!" he said, waving his hand, as if brushing it off. "I don't care! Reed's hurt real bad. Come help me get a tree off him."

"Yeah right... How can I be sure it's not another one of your traps?" I asked as I looked from tree to tree, searching for Reed's movement. "I bet that brother of yours is just waiting to pounce."

He stepped towards me.

"Get back, Parley!"

"I'm serious, Tate. Please—please help me. I'm sorry I called you Rat—out of habit, I guess."

I folded my arms. "What happened?"

"We were trailing you guys."

"Trailing us? What do you mean?"

"Well, you knew where the big white buck was, didn't you? How else was we going to find it?"

I laughed. "So you're lost too?"

"Stop laughing, Tate! I need you now! I know we haven't treated you right in the past, but Reed's going to die if we don't get back. Come on now, the tree's too heavy for me to lift. I've tried everything!"

"I don't know," I said, backing towards the tree, scanning the surrounding forest for Reed's approach. "I don't trust you, Parley."

I can't just forgive. Not after what he's done to my sister, not after what he's done to me...

"You don't deserve forgiveness," I whispered. The words caught in my throat.

Parley's head dropped. "I'm sorry, Tate. I really am," he said, his voice soft.

The Ghost Deer forgave, but why can't I?

My mind flashed back to that day on the playground.

*   *   *

"You leave her alone!" I said, charging over.

Parley let go of her braid. "Oh, now look here, your big brother coming to save you. How sweet."

"You apologize, or you're going to have to answer to me..."

Parley shoved Molly, causing her to stumble into the playground gravel. She looked at her hands and cried.

223

"That's it, Parley! You leave her alone! I don't want to see you touch her ever again!"

"Why should I? You're my friend, aren't ya?"

"Not anymore, Parley! If you're going to treat Molly that way, you're no friend of mine!"

*   *   *

Parley's voice broke. "He's my brother, Tater, he's all I got!" He started sobbing. "Please forgive me," he said, burying his face in his hands. "You've got to believe me. I need your help."

I sighed. *Is he still feeding me a line? I can't trust him, can I?* My heart pleaded with me to help, but my mind couldn't forget.

I felt the tension leave my body, and I folded my arms across my chest. "Why'd you do it, Parley?"

Parley tried to fight back the emotion as he wiped away his tears. "Do what?"

"You don't remember?" I asked, my eyes wide and mouth open.

"Yeah... I've done a lot of things I'm not proud of. I just don't know what you're talkin about—that's all."

"If you want to hurt me—fine. But don't you dare hurt Molly."

"Oh—you're still mad about the playground?"

"Of course! How could you forget that? You really upset Molly; you know that?"

"I'm sorry, Tate... I didn't mean to. I—I—guess I was just hurtin."

"Hurtin? As far as I can tell, you've been the one doing all the hurtin."

"You don't know what it's like."

"To be the bully?"

"No, to have your family ripped apart and your life turned upside down. Mama left us and Dad's a drunk."

I swallowed hard and looked at his pain-filled eyes illuminated in the flashlight. "I guess you're right. I don't know what that's like. But how does hurting people make it better? Why Molly? Why me?"

He looked at the ground and turned, attempting to hide the tear rolling down his cheek. "Because you're the ones I like the most."

"Some way to show it."

"I know… It's just hard, Tater. That day in the playground… Molly wouldn't give me the time of day. I tried everything to be friendly. She just kept ignoring me—like I didn't even matter. I got so sad and frustrated I couldn't take it no more. I just wanted her to like me. That's all."

"Like you?"

"Uh… yeah."

"Why?"

"Well…" He kicked at the dirt. "I don't know. I reckon I like her."

"Gosh Parley, she's my sister."

"Yeah, so what? Anyway, when she stuck her tongue out at me, it was like a punch in the gut."

"It still doesn't make it right. Why did you keep hurting us? Some way to show you like us…"

He sighed and nodded.

"You remember that time Molly and I were fishing, and you smeared mud on her face? You and Reed threw me in the river when I tried to stop you? Do you remember punching me in the stomach after that baseball game instead of giving me a high five? You recall dumping that cup of soda on my head and embarrassing me in front of the whole lunchroom? Do you remember everything else? Do ya!?"

"I know... I know, Tater. After you gave me the cold shoulder and I didn't have any friends, picking on you was the closest thing to a friend I had."

What? All this time Parley's been hurting me because he was lonely?

I looked at the broken shell of my once-friend. Yes, there were some real hat-hanger memories before all the pain. Playing cowboys, romping around the fields, and teaching Bandit how to fetch. How we loved chasing those squirrels and building forts in that patch of trees by the ranch. I remembered the time we built a bull out of that old barrel hanging from the sycamore tree and the time we cooked fish on sticks over the fire like real mountain men.

Those were good times, I thought. *So long ago now...*

"I'm sorry, Parley, I didn't know."

He turned away.

I started walking towards him. "So, all this time you just wanted to be friends?"

"Just go!" he said, waving me off. "No one cares anyway. I've just about lost everyone. Dad's broken, and without Reed, I have nothin. I can't waste more time. I'm going back to help him myself!"

"Forgive me, Parley," I said. "I thought you were feeding me a line."

He looked at me with a tear-streaked face. There was no anger or hatred.

"We used to be friends," he said somberly.

I nodded. "Yes... we were, weren't we—It's been a while, hasn't it?" I asked, putting my arm around his shoulder. "Let's go help your brother."

*　　*　　*

We soon found our way back to Reed, lying on the ground, face pale, with a large aspen tree lying across his chest.

He coughed, wheezing and struggling for breath, as we approached. His eyes were large and white, filled with fear.

"Help," he whispered, attempting to push off the tree. It must have weighed a thousand pounds. My hopes sank at the realization that Parley and I might not be enough.

"Come on, Tate!" Parley yelled, grabbing the trunk.

I jumped in to help, driving my feet into the mud, attempting to secure my footing. Dark sky and falling rain filled my view as I gripped the trunk.

Parley yelled, "One, two, three!"

Rain streamed down my face as I lifted with everything I had. "Aaahhhhh!" I yelled.

Dread filled me. The tree didn't even move. It was no use. Reed was going to die, and there was nothing we could do about it. His eyes looked up at me, pleading. Lightning flashed across the sky, followed by a loud *"boom!"*

Please, Father, I prayed silently. *I know Reed and I have had our differences, but please help him.*

A distant bark rang through the forest.

"That didn't sound like a wolf," I said, looking at Parley.

229

"I don't care!" Parley yelled. "Help me get this off!"

"We tried, Parley! We gave it all we had!" I yelled back over the pounding rain. "I wish we could, really I do—I just don't know what else…"

"Try again!" Parley pleaded, crying out in agony. "Come on, Tater, we've got to do it!"

I sighed, feeling helpless, looking into the showering rain above.

Then, in a flash, I had an idea.

"Quick, help me get a log," I said.

Within moments, we found a downed tree.

"Help me kick off these branches!" I said.

We soon had it cleared.

"Good, now let's take it back to the tree."

Reed's face was white as a ghost, his eyes closed.

"No!" Parley yelled, dropping his end of the log and running towards Reed.

"Hey! What are you doing?" I asked. "Pick it up! Reed needs you."

He nodded.

"Okay now, Parley, shove the end under that tree. See there, use that rabbit hole."

"Here?"

"Yes! Good, now help me pry up on this end."

As we did, the end of the log caught in the hole, acting as a pivot until it contacted the underside of the tree.

"Come on, Parley! It's moving. Lift higher!"

The tree cracked as it rose off Reed's chest. "Higher, Parley! Higher!"

Soon we had the log over our heads, at an angle to the ground. The aspen tree lifted off Reed's chest, sliding down our log with a *"crack! crack! crack!"* breaking off branch stubs along the way, thudding onto the ground beside Reed.

We threw the log onto the grass and collapsed to our knees. "Thank you, God," I whispered. "Thank you."

Parley crawled to his brother. "You okay, Reed? Come on, answer me, brother!" he pled, hugging Reed tight.

I got up, joining Parley, placing my hand on his shoulder. I felt warm inside and couldn't quite tell why. Reed's eyes fluttered open. He smiled weakly.

"Breathe, Reed, just breathe. You'll be alright. Come on. Don't give up on me," Parley said, pushing on Reed's chest.

Reed moaned. "That's—that's one heavy tree," he whispered. He rolled his head to the side and looked up weakly. "Thank you," he said, reaching out.

I took his hand. "Yeah, it was heavy alright."

He coughed, grimacing in pain. "I think I have some broke ribs."

"Probably do. Can you breathe alright?"

Color started returning to Reed's face.

"Yeah, but it hurts."

Just then, barking rang out from the nearby tree line.

I turned. "Hand me the flashlight over there, Parley," I said, pointing at the ground.

I shone the light in the direction of the breaking branches. A dog burst out from under a patch of brush.

"Bandit!" I called out.

He ran across the edge of the meadow. I fell to my knees as he jumped at my chest, knocking me over and licking my face.

"You found me, boy! You found me!"

I heard Dad call out from back in the trees. "Bandit! Bandit! Where are you, boy?!"

Bandit barked, wagging his tail. After licking my cheek, he dashed back into the trees. Soon, Dad emerged with Bandit. I waved the flashlight in his direction.

"Over here!" I yelled.

"Tate! You're alive!" he said, running towards me.

I ran to meet him. Dad was half laughing and half crying as he scooped me up in a big bear hug. "I thought I lost you, bud!" he said, putting my camo hat back on my head.

I smiled. "You about did."

"We saw all those dead wolves back there, found your buck by your pack, believed you were gone for sure."

Just then, Grandpa, Sam and his boys emerged from the edge of the forest, pointing and slapping each other on the back.

"Tater!" Grandpa called out.

I ran up and gave him a big hug.

"You alright?"

"Sure am," I said. "More alive now than ever. All that talk about freedom, Grandpa, and finding my way out of my corner…"

"Yeah, I remember."

"I think I understand it better now."

"Really, that's great to hear, Tater. You sure had me worried. I never dreamed you would leave your buck."

I smiled. "I would for friends," I said, trying to catch the words before they left my mouth. I glanced over at the Bogsleys, wondering if they had heard.

Grandpa's eyes opened wide. "Friends?"

I nodded at Parley and with hesitation swallowed hard. "Yeah—friends."

He smiled and tugged at the brim of my hat. "You seem a little taller, Tater."

I nodded. I felt taller. Something had changed inside of me, and I couldn't quite tell if the old me had broken down or grown up. Maybe a little of both, I reckon.

"How did Bandit get here, Gramps?"

"Your Dad sent Brock and Carter back for him last night when we couldn't find you. We weren't having any luck until they caught up with us bringing that old rascal of yours."

Grandpa pointed at Dad, who was now helping Reed. "What happened?"

"The tree fell on him."

"Well, let's get him home," he said, nodding in his direction. "It appears you have a buck and a friend to pack out, and a bunch of stories to go with it."

"I sure do," I said, smiling. "Turns out freedom is a lot more than I thought, Grandpa."

He chuckled. "Sure is, Tater—it sure is."

EPILOGUE

Several hundred yards away, on a hill across the ravine, the man watched the hunters wearing tree-like clothing load the boy onto the stretcher. Careful not to be discovered, he concealed his red cloak and graying black hair behind a large juniper tree.

Why were these men in his forest, his very lands? That of his grandfather and generations before. Was not robbing them once enough?

Chetona spat on the ground, glaring at the large gray wolf with a scar across his face standing by his side. In a dry gravelly voice he said, "I thought you finished this." He returned his gaze to the men. The creature growled, looking up with menacing yellow eyes.

The old man's voice crackled as he laughed, raspy and callused. "I know, old friend," he said, stroking the wolf's neck. "The White Buck betrayed us yet again. First the trapper, who has become useful to us, yet now these intruders enter our woods. We must put this to an end."

Pausing, he sneered, exposing his rotted teeth. "They cannot know we are here. Like a viper in the tall grass, our secrecy is our greatest weapon. As our rebellion grows, the mountain will be ours shortly. Our brothers within will fall. These white men cannot impede that pursuit."

He patted the wolf's head. "Come, Arakan, we go. This is not the end, but just the beginning."

Thank you for joining us on this journey! If you enjoyed this work and would like to share it with others, please leave a book review. We appreciate your comments and feedback.

THE SAWTOOTH LEGACY SERIES

THE GHOST DEER - Book 1   THE LAST ROUNDUP - Book 2

*Additional Series Books in Development

www.liftingtree.com

Made in the USA
Middletown, DE
22 December 2024